SONS OF THE SPHINX

'We have read of your intended expedition to Egypt, to the Pyramid of Khufu . . . Only death can be your lot if you embark upon this journey. The Sons of the Sphinx.' So reads the sinister message in fine Arabic script mailed to a Hollywood movie producer. But the filming goes ahead — and the body of his chief cameraman is found with his throat cut . . . While in *Corpses Don't Care*, the grand opening of a luxury hotel is ruined by a series of six corpses turning up in the most inconvenient places!

NORMAN FIRTH

◆

SONS OF THE SPHINX

Complete and Unabridged

LINFORD
Leicester

First published in Great Britain

First Linford Edition
published 2016

A catalogue record for this book is available
from the British Library.

ISBN 978–1–4448–2699–9

Published by
F. A. Thorpe (Publishing)
Anstey, Leicestershire

Set by Words & Graphics Ltd.
Anstey, Leicestershire
Printed and bound in Great Britain by
T. J. International Ltd., Padstow, Cornwall

This book is printed on acid-free paper

Contents

Sons of the Sphinx

1

Randall's Last Try

I expect, by the time this gets into print, that most of you will have seen that mighty epic of Egypt and the desert called *Flames of the Pyramids* directed and produced by Maurice Randall of Randall Realm Films. You'll probably also know that the film made millions for its producer, and possibly you'll have remarked on the unusual *acting* capabilities of the small cast — especially when they are supposed to be terrorized by the living mummy of Queen Nep-Tal-Thea.

Well, that *wasn't* acting! They *were* terrified! Every one of us was — terrified of something we couldn't put our hands on; of the strange inexplicable events which happened while that film was being made.

I don't suppose Maurice would ever have gone through with it at all if he'd known what horrors and tragic deaths were to confront our little company. But, of course, he didn't know; and though, in all fairness, we were warned, he laughed that off, as we all did.

It started quite a while ago now — roughly a year. The world was more or less at peace, and those portions of it which weren't, were being rapidly subdued. This didn't affect us much in Hollywood. There might not have been a war on at all — might never have been one as far as Maurice was concerned, for he was Grade 4F. I knew there *had* been a war, I'm sorry to say, only too well. I knew it by the maddening twinges of my game leg where a sniper had pumped four bullets into it. However, it was coming along nicely that day Maurice came into my office, and said:

'Hello, Colin. How's the leg?'

'Passable,' I told him. 'Haven't seen you since the day I got back. What have you been up to?'

He looked gloomily at some papers on my desk, then said: 'I'm in a bad way, Colin. I don't mind telling you this, because we've been friends for a long

4

time — but don't spread it around: the truth is that Randall Realm Films is nearly on the rocks. I've enough left to make one picture, cheaply, and if that doesn't throw them at the box office, I may as well call it a day and go on relief!'

I sympathized with him, for I knew how hard he'd feel this. He'd started his company about three years ago, and at that time he'd stood up fairly well to his rivals, for war restricted raw materials, and films were short. The movies he did make were good — but once peace had come and restrictions been removed, he just hadn't the money to compete with the big companies. I'd seen the crash coming for some time, and I felt partly responsible, since I handled the publicity angle for his studio.

'I'm damned sorry, Maurice,' I told him. 'I've played up every possible stunt to get you more publicity.'

'Oh, it isn't your fault,' he said with a smile. 'I can't compete against the big names the other studios have got. I ask you: what chances do Rodney Strong or Sandra Tate stand against the other film companies' big names? None at all. The only way out is to do something the others aren't doing — and do it good. Make something the public will want to see — as authentically as possible.'

And then he sprung it on me, as suddenly as that. 'That's just what I'm going to do, Colin. And I want your help.'

'In any way I can,' I said sincerely. 'I'm a publicity man, and if there's any putting this new thing of yours over, I'll do it, or break my back trying.'

'I want you to do more than handle the publicity,' he told me. 'You were in Egypt during the war, weren't you?'

'Yes, I was posted there because I speak the language so well.'

'How would you like to go back?'

I shuddered and said fervently: 'Maurice, wild horses wouldn't stand a chance against me. Nothing would make me go back there. I had enough of the place — the flies, the stench in the lower quarters, the heat, the blazing sun! No thanks. I'll take Hollywood, where it does rain sometimes.'

'But I didn't mean to go back to the cities — not places like Cairo and Alexandria.

I meant the desert, in the pyramid belt. It'd be better there, wouldn't it? More peaceful?'

'Peaceful?' I echoed. 'Have you ever been assaulted by a battalion of sand fleas? No? Well, you'll realize what total war is if you ever are.' And I scratched reminiscently at my backside where I myself had suffered. Maurice looked a bit upset, so I slapped his back and said: 'Suppose you tell me all about it before I finally say no?'

He did. He told me everything about it, and I must admit he even instilled some of his own enthusiasm into me.

'I had a screenplay submitted to me by an unknown writer,' he told me. 'I bought it during the war when I had money to spare, for even then the quality of it struck me. It's called *The Mummy Walks*, but I'm changing the name to *Flame of the Pyramids*. That ought to tell you what it's all about.

'Of course, it needs the authentic settings; it's about a bunch of Egyptologists finding the queen's chamber in one of the pyramids, and about that lady coming to life — usual stuff, but wonderfully done. I wanted to make it in Egypt, since there isn't a Californian location which would be quite suitable — but while the war was on I put it to one side. Now we can travel again, I feel I want to make it as a last try to keep the company going. It will need only a small cast; and if I do it in Egypt, using the real thing, I'll save set costs, and I'll get bunches of authentic extras in the shape of natives, for a few cents.'

'Piastres,' I corrected.

'Piastres then. I've enough to get the cast and equipment over there, and I've already written to the Egyptian government and obtained permission to go ahead with my plans. They feel that the picture will be an inducement for more tourists to go over there visiting. The action centres round a pyramid . . . '

'Pyramid? Then those very tourists you mentioned will spoil the idea — they're always haunting the pyramid belt! Especially the Great Pyramid at Giza.'

'I know — and in their letter of permission, the Egyptian government advised me that they would prefer me to use the Pyramid of Khufu.'

'Khufu? I'm darned if I've heard of that one!'

'Probably not. It's about three miles or so from the Pyramid of Djoser, near Saqqara, and from what they say it's pretty similar to that one. Know anything about it?'

'I know the Pyramid of Djoser,' I admitted. 'Been over it. It's known as the Step Pyramid on account of its unusual formation, being a series of five gradually diminishing steps with an excavation in the centre and the King's Tomb entrance below that again. Inside it's a labyrinth of passages and tunnels. And you say this Khufu Pyramid is like it?'

He nodded. 'They say it isn't quite as large, but the architecture is the same. The reason they suggest that one is because it's so far off the beaten track, tourists never visit it. It's deserted.'

'I understand. Yes, the idea's good — but it would probably mean camping out in the desert.'

'I thought that would be rather novel.'

'You did? Just wait, brother, just wait. I'll guarantee we're eaten alive before the movie's half made. You'll see.'

His eyes brightened. 'Then — then that means you'll come along?'

I sighed and nodded. 'If you want me. You'll need one member of the party to speak the lingo. Might as well be me. Business isn't exactly brisk with me at the moment.'

He didn't say anything; just gripped my hand and shook it, but I could tell how much he appreciated my help by the look in his eyes.

And I got weaving the publicity angle right away. He was taking along Sandra Tate as his star, and although I personally didn't like her, Maurice was nuts about her. I posed her for stills in a dainty pith helmet and shorts beside a dummy Sphinx, patting a prop camel. I took glossies of her talking to a bunch of extras made up in long white nightshirts and knotty beards. I took one of her gazing in horror at a papier-mâché mummy. I gave it the works.

The World magazine spread itself with

the material. It ran an eight-page illustrated article entitled: 'STARS OF THE EAST; RANDALL REALM COMP. MAKES BID FOR SUPREMACY WITH EASTERN FILM. STUDIO ONE LOCATES IN EGYPT.'

So that soon everybody knew about it, and the films which were then running currently featuring Sandra Tate and Rodney Strong got a good boosting, and packed them in.

It was a fine start. *The World* printed all the details, and other photogravure sheets followed their example. Swell.

Then one day, just twenty-four hours before we were due to start on the first leg of our journey, Maurice came into my office wearing a very thoughtful frown. He slapped down a piece of paper and a scrap of wood on my desk. The paper was covered with fine Arabic script, and I picked it up and said: 'What the devil's this?'

'You tell me,' he replied. 'I can't make it out. It comes from England, according to the postmark on the package.'

I began to read it, and as I did so my face grew worried.

'We have read of your intended expedition to Egypt, to the Pyramid of Khufu. We now most solemnly warn you that only death can be your lot if you embark upon this journey. We have set our faces against such an enterprise, and our number is legion. We are everywhere and Egypt abounds with us. Again we warn you . . . *Stay away from Egypt and the Nile.* Stay away from Khufu.

The Sons of the Sphinx.'

Maurice's features were a study in bewilderment. He said: 'What kind of damned joke's that?'

I picked up the scrap of sandalwood and studied it carefully. It was carved beautifully in the shape of a small Sphinx, every detail perfect. 'It *may* be a joke — I don't know. It's a pretty awkward time to be going off to Egypt at the moment. The place is alive with terrorist organizations.'

His jaws set stubbornly. 'Well, no damned terrorists are going to terrorize me! I'm going. Let anyone try to interfere with my plans and I'll give *them* Sons of the Sphinx!'

I laughed and slipped the paper and carving into my desk. 'As long as we have this we may as well capitalize on it. I'll give *The World* the story and the carving — they'll jump at it.'

Which is exactly what I did, and within a couple of days the journey to England had completely removed the threat from our minds. But it was due to be brought home to us again, and that very shortly, and unpleasantly!

* * *

We spent a few days in England before embarking on the last lap of our trip. London was much the same as when I had been there two years previously, except that now the lights were up, and the look of strain had gone from the faces of the people who had borne so much of the brunt of Hitler's regime of fear.

By the way of improving the shining hour, we paid a visit to the British Museum, which had just reopened, and spent hours in the Egyptian room. I was particularly interested in the mummified remains — or should I say, rather, petrified? — of a man who crouched against a spur of sandstone, seeking protection from a sandstorm, and had been killed thus. It was while studying this that I noticed the woman.

She was one of those typical English women for whom I have always had a great admiration: flaxen-haired, big blue eyes, and clear skin without a superfluity of make-up. She was hatless and wore a light summer dress of white with a green belt and green collar. Her figure was flawless.

I moved round the case. 'Rather an interesting specimen,' I said.

She nodded pleasantly. 'Yes, it fascinates me. I wonder who the poor soul was — where he was going, and if he suffered much before he died.'

'By the look on his face he suffered a lot, I should say.'

We wandered along to the next case. 'I hope you'll forgive my intrusion on your privacy,' I said.

'Of course. You're an American, aren't you?'

'Yes, I am. Name's Colin Maynard — I'm publicity agent for the film company who're going across to Egypt. You may have heard?'

At these words her gaze had fixed on me, and there was a strange look in her eyes. 'Why, yes, I've heard of you,' she said. 'You've been — threatened, haven't you? Some people called the Sons of the Sphinx?'

'We have — I'd almost forgotten, though. As a matter of fact I'm beginning to think it's all a joke of some kind.'

She shook her head, her blue eyes enigmatic. 'I shouldn't be too sure it's just a joke, Mr. Maynard. If you'll take my advice you'll be very careful on this trip.'

Immediately I was on my guard. 'Do you know anything about the Sons of the Sphinx?'

'I know enough to be aware that they aren't any *joke*. That is all I can tell you.'

She started to hurry off towards the staircase, and I followed her, puzzled. I caught her up at the exit, but she continued to walk on rapidly, down the steps into the street.

'Look here,' I said, a little annoyed. 'If you know anything about these Sons of the Sphinx, the least you could do would be to tell me. If there's any danger it would help us to know.'

'There *is* danger — grave danger. But I can't say anything more. Goodbye, Mr. Maynard.'

'But — but — ' I called, as she climbed into a taxi which had drawn up. 'But see here — '

'And good luck,' she said, closing the door. The taxi crawled out into the main road, leaving me staring helplessly after it.

★   ★   ★

When we had dined that night, Maurice assembled the company in his rooms at the hotel for a final word before we embarked on the morrow. Besides myself there were four cameramen — one of whom was absent, having not returned from a play he had gone to see, as well as Sandra Tate, blasé as ever; Rodney Strong, suntanned and supercilious; Alice Black, the spinsterly wardrobe mistress;

16

and Baxter 'Trix' Cousins, our technical adviser and part-time cameraman. It was with this small company that Maurice planned to produce an epic, and although I doubted his ability to do so, I didn't say anything which might have discouraged him. He spoke frankly and feelingly to us.

'You all know that our studios stand at the crossroads; this one film can make or break us — so it has to make! If it proves to be as big a draw as I hope, there'll be an extra bonus on every thousand dollars' profit it brings in. If not . . . well, we'll all be looking for jobs within a few months. It isn't going to be easy; once we start shooting it'll mean living out in the desert, and that'll be tough. But it has to be done, and I'll make things as comfortable as possible for you all.

'I don't have to remind you of the threat made against us; it may, or may not, be a joke. Colin here met someone today who takes it in deadly earnest — but I won't give my opinion about that. If anyone likes to back out now, they may do so . . . while I can still replace them.'

Nobody moved or spoke and Maurice said: 'Thank you. Finally, I want you all to pull together and help me to put our company back on its two feet; to put — so to speak — our shoulders, not to the wheel, but to the pyramid, and push ourselves back to the top. Remember that this one film play can either ruin us, or put us all at the head of our profession.

'I know I have the best players, the finest cameramen, and the best all-round team I could ask for. Good luck to every one of you.'

The meeting broke up, and I think we all felt we wanted to help Maurice to the utmost. I know I did.

Maurice and I, and Baxter 'Trix' Cousins, acting as technical adviser, sat up late in Maurice's rooms, planning final details of the equipment we would need to take along. Having completed these necessary arrangements, we were thinking of pushing off to bed, when there was a knock at the door.

Maurice opened it, and a stout gentleman with several chins entered. He said: 'I am Chief Inspector Severn from

the Yard, gentlemen. You are Mr. Randall?'
Maurice nodded, and he continued: 'You
had a cameraman attached to your party
called Harry Nesbitt?'

'We have,' agreed Maurice.

Severn shook his head slowly. 'You *had*
— Nesbitt was found in a dark alley
tonight, his throat cut, and a small
wooden sphinx tied to his buttonhole!'

2

The Woman on the Boat-Deck

The murder delayed our departure a further three days, but finally Severn informed us we could not assist by staying any longer, and promised to keep us posted if anything happened, or they came anywhere nearer the discovery of the murderer.

Thursday morning saw us out of the channel, heading on the last lap of our journey to the land of the Sphinx. The sea was calm and smooth, but a sharp wind was blowing from the east; not a cold biting wind, but nevertheless quite sufficiently boisterous.

Trix drifted away to look for the ladies, and Maurice turned to me and grinned. 'Poor old Trix — he'll never bear up for a month or more out at the Khufu Pyramid — unless, of course, we do find a live mummy. That'd console him.'

'Sure,' I agreed. 'And he wouldn't care

much whose mummy it was — nor what Daddy would think. I think I'll take a turn round the boat-deck. Coming?'

He shook his head. 'No thanks. I don't care to move at the moment. Trying to get my sea legs. See you later.'

I nodded and went up to the boat-deck. There were quite a number of passengers up there, taking a constitutional round the rails. The wind was blowing hard, and the ladies were having trouble with hats and dresses. Trix was standing against the rail, holding onto the pork-pie hat he always wore and eyeing the shapely limbs of the women who passed. Trix regarded the wind as a heaven-sent gift that gave him an opportunity to weigh up — as it were — form.

I had covered half the distance round when a large sun-brimmed hat whirled past, and feeling chivalrously inclined I chased it along the deck, just bringing it to a halt as it was about to flop over the rail into the water. I turned with it in my hand to look for its owner, and judged her to be the young lady a few yards from me who was, at the moment, fighting to prevent her dress from being whipped in the air, and revealing a remarkably lovely pair of legs in the bargain. Her face was bent forward, and I could not see it.

I walked over to her, and during a sudden lull in the wind, said: 'Your hat, madam?'

She looked up, and I almost staggered. '*You!*' I exclaimed.

She didn't speak immediately, and I could see she was not as surprised as me. She said: 'I expected to see you on this ship — it's nice seeing you again.'

'Really? I wouldn't have thought you'd have cared to see me again after running away from me outside the museum. I really think you owe me an explanation, don't you?'

The wind rushed about us once more, and she said: 'It's far too windy to talk up here — suppose we go on the lower deck?'

I agreed and we went below. The lower deck was extremely windy also, and we eventually wound up in the saloon, with drinks before us, and cigarettes in our hands.

'Well?' I said.

She tapped her smoke delicately on the edge of an ashtray. 'Well?' she echoed.

'The explanation. Or aren't you giving one?'

'I don't think I need to. I had an appointment and I was in a hurry. That's all.'

'Not quite. How about your remark regarding the Sons of the Sphinx?'

'How about it? I simply warned you to be careful. That's all there is to it.'

'I suppose you know one of our cameramen was murdered in London, presumably by the same merchants?' I demanded.

She looked uneasy, but nodded. 'I know that. I told you to be careful — I can't tell you anything else. If you persist in talking about it I must ask you not to speak to me again, Mr. Maynard. Now what will you do? Forget I mentioned it and be friends while we're here, or insist on arguing with me?'

I shrugged. 'You don't give me much option, do you? Very well, we'll forget it. I suppose you're going as far as Egypt?'

'Yes, Alexandria. Are you?'

'Same spot — so if we're to be acquaintances for that length of time I think I ought to know what they call you.'

'My name's Joan — Joan Kennett.'

'Then I'll call you Joan,' I told her handsomely.

'Oh, *will* you? Just like *that*?'

'Just,' I said, nodding. 'And you, in return, can call me Colin. Or are you going to pull that old English reserve stuff on me?'

She laughed. 'I don't think it would work anyway, would it? All right, Colin. You win.'

'Are you on holiday, Joan?'

She frowned at me. 'If you don't want to ruin a glorious shipboard flirtation, don't ask questions. That's one thing I must insist on: as long as we're on this ship, let's agree not to ask each other anything about each other. For instance, I might ask you all sorts of embarrassing questions, mightn't I? Such as, for example, are you married, engaged, or otherwise tied?'

'I'm not,' I told her frankly. 'I'm

perfectly eligible.'

'I guessed that — but I don't really want to know. I simply want us to agree on one thing — *no questions*.'

'No questions, then,' I said solemnly. 'If you don't want to add anything to your remarks of that other day, you don't have to.'

We talked pleasantly of this and that, and it appeared she had not only been to Egypt before, but also spoke the language like a native. We were soon jabbering away at each other in that tongue, and causing the other passengers to stare at us blankly. When she left me later, I had arranged to dine with her, and afterwards to dance in the main saloon.

As I went to my cabin I passed Trix, who said: 'Hey, pal. How about an intro to that swell lulu you was beating gums with? I guess I could go for that more than slightly.'

'You're too late, Trix,' I said, smiling. 'I've already gone for it!'

★   ★   ★

The main saloon was crowded that first night out; a six-piece band played modern dance numbers and I have never enjoyed a dance more than those I had with Joan. Joan! I liked her name; the way she talked, walked — and everything about her. You could say I was already under the ether. In the short time I had known her, she seemed to be everything I had ever dreamed of in a woman.

She danced wonderfully, her soft, alluring body clinging to mine, so that I forgot the dance floor, and everyone else, and we were alone, floating in a magic world far from reality. Her full, upturned lips smiled at me; her eyes were deep wells of beauty and mystery calling to something, some hidden impulse inside me.

Unwittingly I bent low to kiss those inviting lips; I was entirely carried away by the wonder of her — and she recalled me to my senses with a sharp aversion of her head, and a murmured: 'Colin — Colin, please. Remember there are other people here!'

I flushed a little. 'Joan — it's rather

26

stuffy,' I said. 'How about a walk on deck? I don't like the way that young naval officer's been eyeing you — I've got a notion he's going to cut in any minute.' I nodded towards a chinless specimen with light hair who was standing on one side of the floor, looking at us.

As I finished speaking he began to come across, and Joan said: 'All right, Colin, I'd like some fresh air.'

We wandered out on deck. It was a magnificent night, a large silver moon beaming down on the swelling sea; a thousand stars twinkling in the black above us, like diamonds on velvet. The only sound to be heard besides the throb of the engines was the steady swish of the propellers as the ship cut through the sea.

We leaned against the rails, and somehow we got to talking of our childhoods. I told her of my boyhood ambitions to be a famous actor; how I had crashed Hollywood, and had been lucky to even wind up as a publicity agent. She looked thoughtful and said: 'I've always had an ambition for — adventure. I hate a dull humdrum life, the kind most people lead. I always wanted to get away from that sort of thing.'

'And did you?'

'That's going perilously near to asking questions, Colin. Questions I can't answer. Let's change the subject.'

'To what?' I asked her.

'I don't know — but there are a million things I could think of . . . ' And she smiled up at me.

It was the smile that did it; the smile which snapped the last threads of conventionality in me. I said hoarsely: 'I can only think of — *one!*'

And the next moment she was in my arms, pressed close against me, her lips hard to mine. While she didn't actually struggle against my embrace, she made no effort to return it. She stood silently; still, with her lips warm against my own, her cheek pressed softly to mine. Her hair exuded some faint sweet perfume, and my senses reeled.

I got a grip on myself and released her gently. I felt rather ashamed of myself now — she was certain to think I was a brute, and seven different kinds of a wolf. I stammered: 'Joan — I'm sorry. I'm sorry

I did that — I had no intention of forcing you.'

She smiled at me, and there was something tender in her smile, something which made my heart jump. She whispered: 'Don't be sorry, Colin. I'm not. Life's too short to be sorry about stolen kisses. And you didn't force me, you know.'

'Maybe not — but you didn't exactly jump for joy, either.'

'I know I didn't. But you can't expect any self-respecting girl to throw herself round your neck at the first kiss, can you? No matter how much she wants to!'

I stared at her. 'Then — then how about the second kiss? Would her conscience be eased by then?'

'Why not see, Colin?'

There wasn't any need for further conversation between us. She didn't take the kiss as calmly, either. She returned my embrace, seeming to have cast discretion to the winds, and the warmth and life of her rushed into me, filling me with desire.

We were both a little breathless when we broke away; she straightened her hair,

29

then said: 'Hmm. There mustn't be too much of that Colin, dear. Let's take a stroll round deck to cool off, shall we?'

I nodded, momentarily speechless. We began to stroll round the deck, talking in low tones. It was almost deserted; on the bridge there was life, and we passed an odd steward and one or two sailors. But towards the bows, absolute stillness reigned. We commenced to return the other way, and I spotted a figure leaning over the rails, clearly troubled with shifting cargo. I recognized it as one of our cameramen, and called: 'Having a bad time, Hawker?'

He brought a white, weary face up from over the rail. 'Geez, Mister Maynard, I surely am. Hell, I never woulda come if I'd known it'd be like this — *ULP* — *ulp* — *ullugulp*!' His face shot rapidly over the rail again, and we left him to his misery. We reached the first row of cabins, and in the shadow of the awning paused to look out to sea again.

We had been standing silently there for ten minutes, when a sound from the direction we had recently traversed made us turn and stare down the deck. Hawker, the cameraman we had previously seen, was coming up the scuppers, one hand on the side rail, at a staggering run. He lurched nearer; and now, besides sickliness, his eyes held terror and pain.

I murmured: 'Poor devil — it must be hell to be a bad sailor. Nothing you can do for them, either.'

He had almost reached us, and he now gasped: 'Mister Maynard — I — I — ' A spasm of coughing racked him, and I said gently:

'Take it easy, Hawker. Take it easy, man.'

He opened his mouth to speak; then dumbly, holding hard to the rail, he held out his hand to me and allowed me to see what lay in his palm. *It was a Sphinx!* A small, *sandalwood Sphinx!*

Simultaneously, he collapsed at the knees, buckled forward, and crashed face downwards at our feet. We saw, for the first time, the hilt of an ugly knife protruding from between his shoulder blades!

Joan, in spite of her usual calmness, emitted a thin scream.

In next to no time the deserted deck

was filled with people, all jabbering and shuddering. A tall suntanned man pushed his way through the group to where I knelt over Hawker. He said: 'My name's Harmer — I'm a doctor. What's the trouble?'

He made a swift examination, and when he stood up his eyes were grave. He said: 'This man is dead — stabbed through the heart. Somebody had better call the captain!'

And I looked dully at the little, cursed, sandalwood Sphinx!

3

The Way to the Desert

We held a meeting the next night in Maurice's state room; we were all present — at least, all of us connected with the making of the film — and to us Maurice announced his unshaken determination to go on.

Although the entire company agreed to stick with him, there was a most remarkable lack of conviction in the voices of both Sandra Tate and Rodney Strong. Sandra Tate, when it came to the virtuous and voluptuous heroine of the screen, could face any danger which had been arranged by trick photography, or by stunt takes; so could Rodney Strong. But when it came to actual danger their nerve wasn't quite so good. In fact, I had a feeling then that there'd be trouble in store for Maurice from these two, and I wasn't so far wrong.

33

As regards poor Hawker, well, there was no clue to point to his murderer. The ship was crowded, and any one of a hundred people might have done it. The whole matter was laid aside for the police at Alexandria, and no one was to be allowed to go ashore until the killing had been fully investigated.

We had all sworn allegiance to Maurice, so to speak, when there was a knock at the door, and I admitted the suntanned, tall, middle-aged Doctor Harmer, who had examined poor Hawker. He regarded us all gravely from rimless pince-nez, then said: 'I don't wish to intrude on your privacy . . .'

'You aren't intruding, Doctor,' Maurice assured him. 'Come right in. We were just having a discussion about these murders.'

He nodded. 'That is actually why I came. I happen to have read something of the threat which hangs over you, in the newspapers, and I thought perhaps I could be of some assistance.'

I said: 'Assistance, Doctor? In what way? Do you know anything of these people who call themselves Sons of the Sphinx?'

He inclined his head gravely. 'I have

heard of them — and I have seen some of their victims in the vicinity of the Nile. What they are, who they are, and what their object is, I do not know. But I can assure you they are not to be taken lightly, gentlemen. They are capable of going to great lengths if they have need. There have been dozens of crimes in the last three or four years, all directly attributable to them. I have seen many murdered men — and women — only common natives, but who had known too much, and had been killed and left with one of those small wooden Sphinxes tied to them.'

'You reside in Egypt?' asked Maurice.

'I have my practice there. I suppose, to be immodest, you could call me a Good Samaritan to the Nile natives.'

'You draw your patients from the native population?'

'From the *poorest* of the natives,' agreed Harmer. 'Probably you know the dwellers on the Nile are afflicted by a peculiar complaint of the stomach, occasioned by drinking impure Nile water? It saps their manhood and vitality.

To rejuvenate themselves temporarily, they have been in the habit of taking hashish, which can be obtained easily and cheaply, in spite of the Cairo and District Narcotics Bureau.

'Indeed, by many Nile women it is considered a slight if they are made love to by a man who has not first taken dope! I have done my small best to educate the natives in sterilizing Nile water, and I have given treatment to the more painfully afflicted. It is an ill-paid job, gentlemen, but one which interests me, and occupies all my time. I may add that I am just returning from a visit to my native country, England, for the first time in ten long years, all of which have been spent between Saqqara and Giza. I never expect to see England again. My work now will not be laid aside until I can no longer raise my hand to tend my patients.'

'You certainly are a philanthropist, Doctor,' said Maurice admiringly. 'Few men would devote their lives to such a task, from which they could gain so little.'

The doctor smiled. 'I don't know; I have gained something which is worth far more than wealth in Egypt — the devotion and the love of the natives, who are at heart very loyal. I have won their complete confidence.'

'Except in the matter of the Sons of the Sphinx?' I said.

He frowned. 'Except in that matter, as you say. However, I have not given up hope. I definitely know I have treated members of that very organization, but their lips are sealed tightly. Evidently the least betrayal of their fellows means their death. I still think that someday I shall discover the entire secret and the reason for their formation. At present all I can say is that their numbers include fierce wandering tribes of the Bedouin and Tuareg; fellah from the Delta, the Basin, and the banks of the Nile; and even a number of the native police, who are *not* above bribery. Their members stretch from the wildest wastes of the Libyan Desert to the modern luxury of Alexandria and Cairo. From the Nile Delta to the borders of the Anglo-Egyptian Sudan — perhaps beyond, who knows?'

'Then we surely are facing a whole lot

of risk,' said Maurice slowly. 'I hadn't any idea they were so powerful. Why do you suppose they could be interested in us, Doctor? We aren't trying to harm them, yet they seem so damn keen on warning us off.'

Doctor Harmer shook his head. 'I couldn't give even a faint guess, Mr. Randall. I do know that their influence in Mit Rahina, Tarfa, and other villages and towns surrounding Saqqara, is very strong. And since you gentlemen will be operating in the vicinity, at the Pyramid of Khufu, it is possible they resent it. My advice for you would be to choose some other district, less lonely, for your film making.'

'I'm *damned* if I do,' snapped Maurice determinedly. 'I've had permission to use that pyramid, and from what I hear it'll be just ideal for the film. And by God I'm going to make it there. No half-baked, dirty son of the sand'll stop me, either!'

I saw the expression of pain cross the doctor's features at Maurice's tactless reference to the people the doctor had spent so long amongst as 'dirty sons of the sand'. I coughed warningly, and Maurice said at once: 'I'm sorry, Doctor. I wasn't referring to the people you know and like — merely to the men who are members of this organization.'

Harmer smiled and nodded. 'Don't apologize. I must admit the natives would seem dirty to a European eye — but their dirt conceals qualities which could never be found in a European breast. Their generosity . . . '

'I have always understood they were avaricious?' said Maurice.

'They are,' said Harmer with a smile. 'To the tourist, whom they consider fair game. But not to their own kind.'

He proceeded to give us a brief outline of the various types and characters of natives he knew and worked amongst, and I for one found it most interesting. I pride myself on my knowledge of Egypt and its people. But even I have never been able to delve so completely into native psychology as Harmer had done. When he rose to leave, much later, we shook hands with him with genuine regret, for the ship dropped anchor early next morning, and we were certain to be much too busy answering police questions to see him again. He promised to call and see how we were getting along if he found himself in the vicinity of Khufu's Pyramid any time within the next six weeks, and on that understanding we parted.

I spent the hours preceding our arrival in Alexandria the following morning searching for Joan Kennett. I failed to find her, and eventually a steward informed me she was below deck in her cabin, packing her belongings for disembarkation. I decided it would be as well not to intrude; since no one might leave the ship until after the police had questioned us, I had no fears that I should be unable to find her.

The police arrived in a small motor-boat, soon after we had dropped anchor. A gaudily uniformed native official was in charge, and he fussed about the deck, making a general nuisance of himself.

Clearly he did not wish to take any action until his superior officer had arrived, and he leaned against the rail, idly watching the excited passengers, and occasionally firing a question at the captain or one of the crew. While he was standing there, Joan Kennett approached him, holding two suitcases, and spoke to him rapidly. He asked her a question and she nodded, opened her handbag, took something out, and held it out to him. Then she moved forward and the object was blotted from my view.

I was starting towards the rail to speak to her and suggest we have a parting drink, when to my surprise the official whistled down to the launch, and the woman clambered down the ladder and into the motorboat. The official then dropped her cases after her, the motor roared to life, and the launch drew away rapidly towards the dockside.

I hurried angrily across to the official and snapped: 'I understood all passengers were to be detained pending your enquiries?'

'All passengers are being detained, sair,' he said blandly.

'Then — then how about the woman who just left?' I rapped.

41

He looked puzzled. 'Woman? I beg your pardon, sair; I do not understand you.'

'The woman in *that boat* — don't deny it, I saw her leave.'

He shook his head and said slowly: 'You are mistaken. There was no woman in the boat which just left. See for yourself.'

He pointed and I was barely in time to see the boat vanish from sight behind a warehouse, not heading for the recognized docking point at all. The woman, however, was still in the boat. I said so.

He shook his head. 'You are suffering from hallucinations, sair. I would advise you to wear a sun helmet.'

He broke off as a further launch puttered out into the harbor and made straight for our craft. It drew alongside, and an Englishman in police uniform stepped aboard. Before he had had a chance to speak to his subordinate I stepped forward and said: 'Excuse me. I was under the impression no one was to be permitted to leave the ship until your arrival?'

He stared at me. 'That is correct. Has

someone done so?'

I pointed to the native official. 'I distinctly saw this man allow a young lady to leave.'

The Englishman turned to the other with a grim frown. 'Is this correct, Sufhan?'

The native drew him aside and with a smile began to whisper in his ear. The senior nodded once or twice, then gave a laugh and came over to me, eyes twinkling. I barked angrily: 'I have no idea what the man has said to you, but I repeat I distinctly saw — '

'I know, I know. Sufhan suspects you of having a touch of sunstroke. He assures me no one has left the ship.'

I spun round in search of others to corroborate my story. I could not spot anyone who might have seen the woman go. The senior official said kindly: 'I would advise you to forget the matter, sir. Otherwise Sufhan might well be annoyed at your wild charges, and I should be regretful to have to take any action against you.'

I stepped back in complete amazement, and he ignored me and walked over to the captain. The thought of what the doctor had said about the native police not being above a bit of bribery occurred to me, and I murmured bitterly: 'Apparently that also applies to the officials!'

The idea that Sufhan and his superior might be members of the Sons of the Sphinx struck me, and although I dismissed it as wildly improbable, it was in a very thoughtful and silent mood that I went through the questioning which followed . . .

*　*　*

Alexandria was much the same as I remembered it, and we lost no time in having our equipment loaded onto the train for Cairo. At the station in Cairo we were met by a venerable-looking, white-haired, goatee-bearded old gentleman who introduced himself to us as Professor Clifton Grimm, formerly Inspector-General of Antiquities to the Egyptian Government. The professor was to be attached to our party as chief technical adviser, and he seemed to be an intelligent and level-headed old fellow, if somewhat advanced in years.

He had been arranging our expedition

during our journey out, and he now told us all he was ready for a leisurely cruise down the Nile to Tarfa, which was the most accessible point to the Pyramid of Khufu. The journey was to be undertaken in a flat-bottomed craft like a flat iron, which the professor had hired for us. Since we had so much equipment he had thought this would be the better method, for the railroad did not welcome heavy additional loads at a few days' notice, and in any case the scenery along the Nile fully justified the voyage by boat.

He had hired a competent dragoman by the name of Yusef, whom we at once nicknamed 'Joe'; a number of mules and camels, which were awaiting us at Tarfa; and a dozen fellah, which would be all the natives we needed to make the picture. Should we require any more, he assured us that for a few piastres each we could have hundreds on the spot within an hour or two. He was right, too; I have found out that you have only to jingle a few piastres in the middle of an apparently deserted stretch of desert, and within two seconds you are besieged by an army of guides, beggars and similar riff-raff.

Maurice had not previously told me that the professor was to be one of our party; accordingly I took him aside that night after we had dined at Shepheard's, and broached the subject.

'I understand when you asked me on this trip, that it was because you wanted someone who could sling the gab with the natives?'

'That's right, Colin. I did. Why?'

'Then how about this Professor Grimm?' I said reproachfully.

He laughed and slapped me on the back. 'Sorry, Colin. The truth is I just wanted you along anyway. I thought you'd be more likely to come if you thought you were indispensable. And you did.'

He was so sincere about it that I couldn't remain annoyed; I did have the feeling that I was a useless passenger, being carried along for no purpose — but the thought that I might be of some help later in the expedition consoled me a little.

We embarked early the following morning at Cairo, and since Maurice expressed a fervent desire to see the Great Pyramid and the Sphinx, we left the boat in charge of the natives and Grimm, while the rest of us disembarked a few miles down the Nile and went by train to the pyramids, roughly four miles away. It was crammed with tourists, and the journey was most unpleasant; furthermore, when we reached the spot, the sand was absolutely black with guides and dragomen, donkeys and mules, camels and visitors.

In spite of the mob scene, however, there was no getting away from the majesty of those massive monuments to the dead. The Great Pyramid of Cheops towered four hundred and fifty feet into the still, hot air, and although its outer covering had been spoiled and torn away by Arabs in the seventh century and after, it was still a thing of majesty and power. Eighty million cubic feet of solid masonry, hauled — not by slaves as is supposed — but by the combined efforts of a great people, as a token of thanksgiving and loyalty to a ruler who was kind, and led wisely.

We walked round the pyramids and

soon reached the feet of the Sphinx. Here, even Maurice had nothing to say. There were natives at work, moving the shifting sand which continually buries portions of the gigantic statue, but even these could not detract from the calm dignity and power of that part-lion, part-human form born from the solid rock and standing a full hundred and seventy feet in height and a hundred feet in length. We walked round it and came back to the face with its badly chipped nose and its expressionless yet enigmatic stone eyes, gazing unseeingly across the desert sands. It seemed to subdue Maurice, for from talking incessantly he now drifted into brief remarks at lengthy intervals.

I took from my pocket one of the small wooden Sphinxes which we had found on the body of Hawker, and we compared it with the original. It was perfect in every detail, even to the chipped nose!

The rest of the party were still at the Great Pyramid, and I led Maurice towards the Rock Tombs of the Fourth and Fifth Dynasties, which were quieter, and freer from the inevitable tourists.

There was one in which I was particularly interested — a tomb in a bad state, but with an interesting hieroglyph on the wall of the outer chamber. We went into this, and I pointed out to Maurice the excellent carving of Hathor.

It was dark inside the tomb, for it was not important enough to be provided with electricity, as so many of them are. We had only my torch to see by, and at first I thought we were alone. *It was then I saw the figures...*

4

The Attack in the Tomb

The figures were four in number, and as I glimpsed their outlines against the glow of the tomb entrance far up the sloping passage, I immediately grasped Maurice's arm and said: 'Look out, Maurice. Someone's sneaking along here . . . '

'Sneaking?' he gasped.

'Just that — whoever they are they certainly aren't *ordinary* tourists. I haven't heard a sound, yet I distinctly saw them entering the passage.'

'But what makes you think . . . '

'The silence, that's all. Why should four people, whoever they are, sneak in a place like this?'

He tensed by my side, and I suddenly swivelled my torch and directed it along the passage. The four intruders were caught in its glare, about twenty feet from us. They were natives, dressed in working costume, and apparently not out of the ordinary in any way. But I was still suspicious. I called: 'Hello, there?'

Now that they had been exposed they walked forward openly, until they were no more than six feet from us. They didn't answer my call, but instead drew slowly and steadily nearer, and now I noticed their hands were on the sashes they wore, holding ready the hilts of long knives, the blades of which were hidden in the folds of their baggy trousers.

Again I grated: 'What the devil do you want? What are you doing here?'

Still they maintained that dead silence; still they advanced, imperceptibly, an inch at a time.

'Get ready,' I whispered to Maurice. 'They're going to attack!'

'Good God!' he exploded. 'Not here — not now! They can't!'

'Can't they? I think they can. A shout wouldn't be heard from here — this tomb is isolated from the rest, and attracts very few travellers anyway.'

We put our backs to the wall, clenched our fists, and waited. Maurice chanced a call for help nevertheless, and his voice roared out through the gloom of the tomb, echoing about the walls.

Then the four natives had their knives out, and without changing expression, advanced upon us. I had the torch to use as a weapon; Maurice picked up a portion of broken rock, and was prepared to sell his life dearly. He may have been unfit for the army, but that there was little wrong with his cool courage I could now see.

Then they were on us, and my first grim swipe had laid low one of them; Maurice hurled his rock into a second man's face and he staggered back, half-blinded, knife falling from his fingers. I scooped it from the floor, and turned just in time to deflect the downward blow of the third man.

He never recovered from that downward stroke; my newly found knife swept up and disembowelled him neatly.

I turned quickly, and saw Maurice sweating with strain as he tried to hold his opponent's knife-hand away from him. I reversed my torch which I held in my left hand and crushed it down upon the skull of the attacker. He crumpled up, curled floorwards. But before I could turn, a savage kick from one of the others who had now recovered jolted into my groin, and I slumped down gasping. Maurice, still on his knees, received similar treatment.

The fellow I had knifed was squirming on the floor; the man I had just struck with my torch lay still and senseless; but the other two were still in the game, and I shuddered in spite of my agony as their swarthy, thin-lipped features bent over me, and a knife was raised . . .

A second and the blow would have fallen; but just at that crucial moment, the fellow's arm was wrenched savagely backwards, and the knife was twisted from his grasp. Strong arms seized the two thugs, and dark faces peered down at us; we were helped to our feet, still groaning.

'By God,' said Maurice wheezily. 'We nearly had it that time. How did you chaps happen along?'

The four native policemen smiled, and the foremost said: 'We are from the police post near the Great Pyramid. Some tourists tell us they hear calls for help from this tomb, so we come. It is lucky we do so. You know who these men are?'

I shook my head. 'No, we don't. But I feel sure they aren't the usual robbers. And if I were not,' I went on, suddenly stepping forward and jerking something from one of the thugs' hands, 'this would convince me that their intention was cold-blooded murder!'

They all stared at the tiny carved sandalwood Sphinx which I held exposed. The native policeman gasped: 'The Sons of the Sphinx!'

He turned to the captives and fired questions at them so rapidly even I could not pick up the gist properly. However, it seemed he was asking them if they were members of the organization known as the Sons of the Sphinx, and both men shook their heads sullenly.

'You lie!' roared the policeman wrathfully. 'You are like the others of your members we have captured — you will not talk. But this time . . . Effendi, you will please lend me your heavy torch?'

I nodded and handed it to him, and with calm brutality he set about his prisoners, not desisting until they lay battered and feeble against the side of the tomb. Then he again questioned them: 'You are Sons of the Sphinx? Otherwise how did you get this carved replica?' he barked at them.

'We found this,' said one of the thugs weakly. 'We found this in a Bedouin tent which we robbed.'

The policeman spat on their recumbent forms, kicked them, and barked to his companions: 'Remove the swine. They will not talk — perhaps they will talk at Cairo.'

He regarded the man I had knifed. 'That is good,' he said coolly. 'This one you have killed. One desert louse less with which we have to deal. By the way, Effendi . . . ' Here he regarded me meaningfully, ' . . . you will not mention the way I have handled these men? I had thought I might get something out of them — I might have known better. It would go hard with me if it was thought I had beaten them up thus.'

'But won't *they* report you?' I asked him.

'Not them — I will insist that they sustained their injuries in the fight which they put up, you see? You will substantiate that story?'

I nodded. He thanked me and went on: 'My brother Amin was also a member of the police. Last year he was found dead, with a little wooden Sphinx pinned to him — now you realize why I was brutal with these men?'

'I realize that,' I agreed, 'and I feel we are in your debt. Perhaps you won't be offended if . . . ' I handed him a handful of coins, and he smirked and said: 'Effendi is very kind. It is a trait I have noticed in many Englishmen, this generosity.'

'We're Americans,' I told him.

He bowed. 'Then you are even more generous, Effendis. We thank you.'

Maurice said: 'Forget it. We're sorry we didn't have more on us. We value our lives at more than a few piastres — if you'll leave me your name and address I'll see you're sent a reward.'

I translated to the policeman, and he flashed white teeth at us and rapidly gave us his address. Then he accompanied us from the tomb, saying we could wash and dust up at the police post.

Rodney Strong, the cameraman, and Sandra Tate had gathered outside the tomb, together with many other tourists. Practically everyone in the vicinity knew something was amiss now, and Sandra Tate's features wore an expression of terrible dread. As we walked down to the police post, she said to Maurice: 'What — what happened?'

'We were attacked,' he told her shortly. 'The Sons of the Sphinx again — they tried to kill us.'

I saw her hands clench. 'Maurice — do you think it's quite *wise* to — to carry on?'

'You know my views on that subject, Sandra,' he told her. 'They haven't changed any yet.'

She tightened her lips and said nothing more. But I saw the way she stared fearfully at the ruffian thugs in the police post, and the shudders that shook her when she beheld the blood stains on my hands.

I was never so glad to wash those same hands; I'm not used to murdering people, no matter how much they ask for it. I admit I had just returned from a war, but my part had been mostly inactive. Any killing I had done had been done always from a distance, and had not been brought home forcibly to me. This was different. In the heat of the moment it had been the natural thing to do; now, looked at in the calmer light of the aftermath, it seemed to me I had been incredibly callous and vicious.

Two hours later saw us leaving the Great Pyramids on the same train which carried the defeated murderers to justice. And half an hour after that saw our boat putting out into the Nile on the last stages of our journey to Saqqara and the tomb of Khufu.

* * *

'Seen Sandra?' asked Maurice, joining me at the rail, and wearing a puzzled look. 'I can't spot her anywhere.'

I shook my head. 'I haven't seen her since we came aboard. Isn't she down in the cabin?'

'No. That's the queer part of it. She isn't anywhere at all. I've been all over the boat — what there is of it — and I can't find a trace.'

We were sliding past a village near the first elbow of the Nile; both Maurice and I had been busy in the cabin, boosting our spirits with some of the whisky which Professor Grimm had been thoughtful enough to include in our supplies. Now we felt much better, and had come up for a stroll on deck. Maurice had left me and gone to look for Sandra, of whom he was very fond, although he concealed the fact. Now he was back, having been unsuccessful in his search.

It was at this moment that Professor Grimm joined us, and handed Maurice a mauve-tinted envelope embossed with the initials S.T. This we both recognized at once as Sandra's stationery. Maurice frowned. 'What's this, Professor?'

'Er — the — young woman — the — er

— leading lady,' said the old professor. 'She left the boat shortly before we sailed from Giza — she told me she was going on by train and would join us at Saqqara. She said you knew about it, and asked me to give you this.' He indicated the letter.

Maurice gasped. '*What?* Where was I at the time?'

'I believe you were imbibing whisky.'

Maurice cursed and ripped open the flap. His eyes raced down the hurried scrawl, then he handed the note to me with a groan. I read it quickly, and gave an angry exclamation, for Sandra had calmly walked out just like that! It said:

'Darling Maurice,

Do forgive me for doing this, but I can't help it, honestly I can't. It's too terrible, really it is. All these murders, and if you don't value your skin, I do mine. I have my public to think of, haven't I? You can't expect me to throw my life away, I mean, can you? Of course you can't. But I know you'd only argue if I told you, so I'm sneaking off the boat and taking the train back to

Cairo. You can have my large luggage sent to the hotel there, and I'll arrange for them to forward it. Goodbye Maurice, dear — see you back in Hollywood.

Love, Sandra.'

'Well,' I grunted, folding the note, 'I expected something like this — and if I were you I'd also keep an eye on Rodney Strong. He hasn't the nerve of a sewer rat, either.'

'You can't blame her in a way,' mused Maurice. 'After all, I haven't any right to ask her to risk her life, have I?'

'Maybe not, but you gave her a chance to back out in London. Why should she have come all this way, when it's too late to get a replacement? How are you going to fill her spot?'

'We'll have a look round in Saqqara — see if we can spot any pretty English or white women there. It doesn't need a lot of acting ability for the part.'

'And if you can't?' I demanded.

'Then I'll cut the damned woman's part out altogether,' he growled. 'I'm just as glad to be rid of her, believe me.'

He tried to sound sincere, but he failed. Only I knew how much he had thought of Sandra Tate — I honestly think he wanted to marry her, and though he hadn't said as much, I suspected she had turned him down more than once. It was the way she treated him with a kind of tolerant condescension that made me suspect this, for a woman of Sandra's type always regards a man she has refused with a mixture of boredom and affection. He is a conquest of the past — another link in her chain of shattered hearts. That was why I had never liked her much; she was the type of woman who lived for what she herself could get out of life, and not what she could give to others.

She was gone, and I was glad of it. Her going presented almost insurmountable difficulties, however, for in spite of Maurice's casual remark to the effect that he would cut the woman's part out of the screenplay, he knew this was impossible. The story centered on a mummy coming to life — and the mummy of a young and beautiful woman at that.

I mentioned this to him, and he said: 'We'll manage. If I can't get hold of a white woman, we'll find some good-looking native. That'll be even better for the purpose. We can teach her all the words she'll need to know — there isn't much talking to the part.'

I didn't disillusion him; I didn't tell him that only one in a thousand Egyptian-born woman could be described as good-looking from a western point of view, and that he wasn't even likely to find that proportion in Saqqara.

He went moodily off by himself to the stern soon after, and I watched the passing panorama under the big, clear moon of an Egyptian night. At ten thirty by my watch, we moored against the bank of the river, a stone's throw from Tarfa.

5

The Place of a Million Dreams

Every one of our tiny company was already suffering from the terrible strain of not knowing what would happen next. When they learned of Sandra's disappearance they expressed surprise and scorn, but the look in Rodney Strong's eyes told me he wished he'd thought of doing likewise. In fact, the most composed of that party was the elderly and prim wardrobe mistress, Miss Black. I really think we had her to thank for averting a good many squabbles, and possibly some hysteria; for when a plain elderly spinster takes a matter of being faced with deadly danger as something not to get too worried about, her male companions can hardly show any signs of the white feather.

While Professor Grimm and Maurice were arranging final details in Tarfa, Trix approached me and said he'd like to visit Saqqara, which was easily accessible. I questioned Maurice, and he said that we would probably have some delay before starting for the pyramid, and I could go ahead. He himself preferred to remain and help Grimm, but really I could see he was in no mood for pleasure jaunts; Sandra's dirty method of letting him down had upset him more than he cared to say.

Bob Lieberman, our other cameraman, attached himself to Trix and me, and the three of us set out for Saqqara soon after breakfast the following day. Trix had proposed that we travel on camels, as he had always wanted to ride a 'ship of the desert', and although I thought he'd find it damned rough riding, I didn't spoil his fun — the camel would do *that*, soon enough.

We found a native stables, and hired the camels; a guide went with them, and he brought the beasts out and bowed to us. I had ridden a camel many times before, and had no difficulty in falling into the habit of mounting again. The camels knelt and I got on and held tight while mine had lurched upright. Bob Lieberman was lucky with his, too, and although he clung for dear life, he managed to stay on.

Not so Trix; when Trix's camel had been brought out, it had looked at the little cameraman with an eye which seemed to say: 'Hmm! Just about my size!' It then opened its jaws and gave a slavering croak.

Trix eyed it warily; the camel eyed Trix. It was apparent that here was no case of love at first sight!

Having seen us successfully mounted, Trix grinned feebly, climbed astride the camel's back, and feeling more secure, waved to us. It was a fatal mistake, for at that instant the native goaded the beast to its feet, and Trix, off balance, described a wonderful somersault in the air and came to rest on his rear in the sand. He looked so rueful I couldn't help laughing, and to add insult to injury the camel glared down at him and suddenly gave voice to a series of grunts which sounded for all the world like laughter. That was the end of Trix and his camel. The camel was taken back to the stables, and a sedate mule was brought in its place. With this Trix had no trouble, and soon we were on our way.

I had only once been in Saqqara, but I remembered a native café there where occasionally Ouled Nail dancing girls gave displays. I took my two companions to this place and secured a corner table out of the way of the motley crowd of natives, Arabs and fellah, who squatted cross-legged on the floor.

The dancing girls gave a good show, and had their faces been in keeping with their bodies, I have no doubt Trix would have been fascinated; but unfortunately they weren't. And since Trix was not in the least interested in the artistic value of the dance of the Almeh, he started drinking rather heavily, a sweetish potent concoction for which the place was noted.

It may have been all right for the natives, who were used to it; but Trix and Lieberman were soon looking the colour of green cheese, and before half an hour had elapsed they made a beeline for the street, holding their mouths. I sat on and waited for them to get over their sickness.

They had been away only ten minutes or so when from the hotel part of the café, which catered for tourists and visitors, a young white woman walked towards the door and into the street. I knew her at once — it was Joan Kennett, who had so mysteriously obtained permission to leave the ship at Alexandria when everyone else had to be questioned!

I laid a few piastres on the table and walked quickly after her. From a narrow street by the café came loud gulping noises, and as I passed I noticed Trix and Bob leaning against the rail, having a hell of a time of it. I cut down there and said: 'Listen — I have to leave you for a while. Go back to the café and wait there for me.'

Unable to speak, they just nodded, and I rushed away, hoping I hadn't lost sight of the woman.

She was still there, heading towards the dirtier quarters of the place, winding through squalid streets of sand and mud huts, going ever deeper into the native district proper. I had to admire her nerve. For a white man to brave those streets, even in daylight, requires courage; but for a white woman, at whom salacious glances are cast by dirty ruffians, and jeering remarks of an obscene nature are hurled, it requires nerves of steel.

She paused before a disreputable eating house, hesitated outside as if uncertain, and then went in. She spoke to a rascal who was evidently the proprietor, and he nodded, leered at her, and waved his hand expansively.

Money changed hands, and the woman sat down on a small stool, took a briefcase from under her arm, and extracted a large drawing pad and pencils.

So she was an artist? An artist in search of fresh and original views and settings? Or *was* she?

She began to sketch rapidly, paying no attention to the lewd eyes of the few customers in the place. Her pencil flew over the board.

After a time the patrons of the eating house lost interest, and returned to their conversations and food. The woman sketched on, but her eyes were alive and alert, darting here and there, and I gained the impression that she was listening to the talk rather than concentrating on her work.

I decided there was nothing to be gained by waiting, so I moved aside the reed curtain and entered. She had no idea I was there until I tapped her on the shoulder; then she jumped as if she had seen a ghost, and whirled about.

'Oh!' she gasped. 'Mr. Maynard!'

'Still Colin to you, Joan,' I told her.

'But what are you doing here?'

'I might ask you a similar question. This isn't any place for an unescorted lady — especially such an attractive one.'

She indicated her drawing board, on which a passable charcoal sketch was taking shape. 'I should think you could see what I'm doing here.'

'You take a lot of risk for authenticity,' I told her. 'If I were you I'd stay in my hotel and work from imagination.'

She shrugged and continued to sketch. 'And what are you here for?'

'I followed you. There's a little matter which I think could be cleared up between us.'

'But Colin, I told you distinctly when you were on the ship that we were only friends for the voyage. Surely you aren't going to make a big romance out of a shipboard flirtation?'

'Not if you don't wish me to,' I replied, a little hurt. 'But really it wasn't that at all. I was referring to your being able to leave the ship as you did — *without being questioned*.'

She stopped drawing and looked at me. 'You saw that?'

'I did. It seemed to me you bribed the Egyptian official.'

She smiled reflectively. 'Yes, I expect it would look like that to anyone who didn't know . . . '

'Didn't know what?' I put in quickly.

She shook her head. 'I've no more intention of telling you that now than I had on the ship. Please don't ask me again.'

I was nettled at her calm assumption that I was just being nosey. I grunted: 'That's all very well, but one of our cameramen was murdered on that ship, and I don't see why you should have left before being questioned.'

'Do you think I committed the murder?' she said levelly.

'Of course I don't. That's ridiculous. How could you when you were with me at the time?'

'Then why was it so essential for me to be interrogated?'

'Well, if you put it that way I suppose it wasn't. But at the same time I don't see why . . . '

'I expect not. But take my word for it that I had nothing to do with the murder, and that I had a very good reason for leaving the ship.'

'I still think — ' I began, then stopped, for she was looking at me, and her cool eyes were now hot and angry.

'Colin, I shall get *really* angry with you in a moment. You're attracting attention to us — now please go and leave me alone!'

'But you shouldn't be alone here . . . '

'I'm fully capable of taking care of myself,' she snapped. 'Now please leave me alone. I didn't ask for your protection.'

I rose stiffly and said: 'Oh, very well. If that's the way you feel, I'll get along. Goodbye.'

'Goodbye,' she answered, already busy with her sketch again; and, feeling more than a little crushed, I withdrew with as much dignity as I could.

★   ★   ★

I had only gone as far as the end of the street when that quality known as chivalry made me stop and think. I didn't like leaving her there without an escort, no matter how confident she was of taking care of herself. I hadn't liked the way the natives had eyed her. Besides — and here I was admitting something to myself which hadn't struck me before — I was very fond of her. *Very*. I wouldn't actually say I was in love — but I had the feeling I was going to fall at any moment. I couldn't go on and leave her there.

Her sketch had been almost finished when I had left, and she could not be long now. I decided to wait for her and apologize for my nosiness, and ask if I could see her again sometime. I hung about the corner of the street watching a number of tattered little children at play, and reflecting that they were not so very different from kids all over the world.

And then I had reason to thank my lucky stars I could speak their native tongue. For they were playing a game which interested me greatly — a game which appeared to be the equivalent of 'cops and robbers' to them. Three of them were lined up against the far wall; three more were advancing upon them with cries of, '*Sons of the Sphinx arise!*'

I tensed and my attention became glued to the game. The three against the wall held their hands as if they were firing rifles; and then their attackers were upon them and they were forced to the ground, invisible knives driven into them, and pushed aside. These three were now, apparently, 'dead'.

The representatives of the Sons of the Sphinx then gave a cheer and turning to a small girl who sat cross-legged on the sand, they prostrated themselves before her.

'They are all dead, Queen Cleopatra,' said the leader of the boys. 'Once again you rule Egypt!'

I was about to step forward and enquire where they had learned their game, when a stout, perspiring native woman dashed into the road, collared two of the boys and the girl, and shrilled: 'Mustapha! Ali! Neenas! How often have I told you not to play *that* game! Come in quick!' And with a fearful glance about, she dragged them into one of the homes.

The remaining four had taken to their heels on her appearance, and now the street was empty, except for an unkempt beggar trudging along with the aid of a staff. I muttered a few swear words under my breath. I thought I might have found out quite a lot from those Arab urchins, and now the chance was gone. I resumed leaning against the wall behind me.

After half an hour had passed, I began to get impatient. Had she started another sketch, perhaps? Was she going to stay there all day sketching? I remembered Trix and Bob waiting for me at the café, and I decided I would walk back and see if Joan showed any signs of leaving.

I did so. I parted the curtain again and stepped inside. The eating house, except for a few customers, was deserted. Of the woman there was no sign! Amazed, I motioned to the proprietor. He hastened forward, and I said: 'The white lady who was here — where is she?'

He looked bewildered. 'What white lady, Effendi? There was no white lady here.'

It seemed that I was always destined to be made a fool of when I enquired after Joan. I snapped: 'Oh, yes, there was. She was sitting on a stool near the corner there.'

'Stool?' said the proprietor blankly. 'Stool, Effendi?'

I gazed round in search of the stool; it was not there. The proprietor turned to the patrons and said: 'Brothers, there has been no lady here, has there?' They chorused their agreement. He turned to me again and spread his hands. 'You *see*, Effendi?'

I rapped: 'I'd like to look upstairs, if you don't object?'

'But certainly not. It is only another room which I share with my family. This way, Effendi.'

He led me up the rickety steps, into a loft-like room. Save for a young Egyptian girl reclining half-naked on a bed, and an old woman sweeping with a broom of twigs and palm leaves, the place was deserted. The proprietor smiled ingratiatingly. 'My wives, Effendi. Old Nali is not fit for much but the housework now; and the other is Gila, my youngest wife. You can see there is no white lady here.'

He led me down to the lower room, and without questioning him further I left. I knew it was useless in the face of such opposition to insist she had been there. The natives stick closer than brothers against a white man.

I circled the place cautiously; at the back there was a mud archway leading to a second domicile. I wondered if the woman had been taken through into this. There was a door round the side, and a sign in Arabic, a literal translation of which would have been 'The Place of a Million Dreams'. I was still standing undecided, when from a window above my head came a sharp crack, like that of a whip, and the scream of a woman in awful torment!

I waited no longer; by bunching myself tautly I was able to spring into the air and just get a grip on the ledge of the hole in the wall which served for a window. I drew myself up slowly and gazed down into a long room full of fumes.

It was a typical dope den, where the natives came to enjoy drugs in convivial company. There was one old man in attendance, and a few hashish-addled natives lying round the place. Beyond these was yet another door of heavy wood, and as I watched there was a further scream of pain, seeming to come from directly behind that door!

I had to take a chance, and drawing myself onto the window ledge I eased through the two-foot square hole, hung by my fingertips, and dropped the remaining five feet to the floor. I landed lightly, and the doped customers had not then noticed me at all. Like a shadow, I sped through that darkened room towards the far door.

The old man looked up as I passed him, and his mouth opened for a shout.

It was never uttered; my bunched fist smacked into his rotten teeth, and he keeled backwards among the debris of the filthy floor. Then I was at the door, had swung it open, and stepped into a smaller room.

I took in the scene instantly: Joan stripped partially naked and tied by wrists and ankles to hooks protruding from the walls, face inward. A burly brute clad in only a loin cloth stood behind her; in his right hand was a long curling whip, which was raised to deliver another stroke on the back of the defenceless woman; already three blood-red weals stood lividly out where the whip had fallen.

Seated to one side was an Arab in a burnoose and robes. He was small, with a dark beard and fierce black eyes. He was watching the sobbing woman curiously, as if waiting for her to speak.

All this I noticed at once; then I had slammed the door after me, twisted the heavy key in the lock and launched myself at the Arab.

He had no chance to resist; the attack was so sudden that he was pulled upright and thrown bodily towards the man with the whip before either one of them had recovered from their surprise. The impact forced them both to the floor, and my flailing boots against their heads did the rest. The Arab collapsed at the first kick; the brute required three before he was out.

Panting from my exertions, I bent down and relieved the Arab of a knife and an old-fashioned carbine which, I noted, was loaded. I swung the knife through Joan's bonds and caught her as she fell limply into my arms. She was still conscious, but her face was strained and grey, and as her back touched my arm she winced and bit her lip.

'Can you stand?' I said quickly, and she nodded. Leaving her leaning on the wall, I retrieved her clothing from a corner where it had been thrown, and handed it to her. She was in too much pain to be worried by her unclad state, or to resent my helping her to dress.

Now there was a hammering at the

door I had locked, and I guessed the old man I had struck had found reinforcements. The brute was stirring again, and groaning. I looked at Joan's white face, thought of the red marks on her white back, and a wave of savage bloodlust swept over me. I picked up the whip from where it had fallen, swung it high, and sent it hissing down across the brute's body. He twitched in agony and screamed. Again and again I lashed brutally at his great body, until he was a writhing, moaning wreck. Then I advanced to the door, cautioned Joan to keep close behind me, turned the key and stepped back.

Three men rushed in, amongst them the proprietor of the eating house. When they saw the Arab's gun levelled at them they paused and gasped at me, then at the writhing brute.

'Get back against that wall,' I growled, waving my gun; and after seeing the murderous look in my eyes, they hurriedly obeyed. With one arm supporting Joan I moved towards the door, holding the key in my left hand.

Joan whispered: 'The other room is

empty except for the ones who are drugged.'

We stepped back, shut the door, and turned the key on the three in the inner room. We picked our way across the recumbent bodies and made for the door.

The old man I had previously struck came dashing from a patch of shadow suddenly, waving an ugly kriss.

There was no help for it; we could not afford to be delayed now, for anything. I pulled on the trigger of the old gun, and smoke and flame spurted round my hand. The old man shrieked, clutched his chest, and thudded to the floor, squirming.

The outer door was invitingly unlocked. Within seconds we were in the street, and I was wondering which way we should go.

The carbine I held was useless now. Its one charge was spent on the old man. Holding Joan tightly, for she was still unsteady on her feet, we started running. We had gained the corner when the rear doors of the eating house opened, and five or six men looked through. Their eyes fell on us, and with a yell they took up the chase.

How long we ran I don't remember — through winding, twisting lanes, past unkempt taverns and cafés, seeming never to reach a more healthy portion of the town. And always behind us came that yelling bunch of demons . . .

We turned haphazardly into a narrow alley and ran along it for ten or fifteen yards. Joan was now close to collapsing point, but I urged her on, helping her as much as I could. And then I saw the *blank wall* looming up ahead!

We were in a cul-de-sac, and as I gasped in dismay, the sound of the yelling mob converging on the alley grew louder . . .

6

Last-Minute Rescue

As we stood there, not knowing which way to turn, Joan's legs gave out under her, and she hung limply from my arm. I picked her up and stared frantically round me. The only concealment of any kind was a dark doorway in the wall of the building to my right. Into this I moved, propped Joan against the doorway behind, and hammered for admittance. Peering from cover I saw the pursuers, now numbering about ten or eleven, surge into the top of the entry . . . it was only a matter of seconds now. When they saw the apparently deserted cul-de-sac they hesitated; but one of them called:

'Perhaps they are hiding somewhere — we will search.'

I wielded the gun I had taken from the Arab. A pocket carbine which didn't work wouldn't be much use against that rabble, but it was better than no weapon at all, and I was determined to down two or three of the ruffians before we were taken.

They began to stream down the entry, searching every doorway. Another twenty seconds, and . . .

The door behind me *opened!*

Joan flopped weakly backwards into the interior of the house. I was gripped by the collar and pulled into darkness. The door slammed again, just as the mob outside drew level.

'Quiet!' hissed a voice speaking in English. 'Wait until they have satisfied themselves you have gone.'

We all remained silent while the cries of the pursuit swelled outside, then gradually died away. At length a match flared, and the light was touched to an oil lamp.

'*Doctor Harmer!*' I gasped, eyeing the old doctor, who was bending over the lamp.

He turned and looked at me. 'Good Heavens! It's Mr. — er — Randall, isn't it?'

'Not far off,' I agreed. 'I'm his publicity manager, Colin Maynard. But I must say

I was never so glad to see a friendly face before in all my life. Another minute, and . . . ' I shuddered.

'I heard your knocking,' he explained, 'and saw the mob turn into the street from the top window. I hastened down to admit whoever was being pursued. It is quite a shock to me to realize what might have happened had I assumed it was merely some common thief or beggar, and not bothered to admit them. Thank God I was in time. But your friend — the lady — she has fainted.'

I looked down at Joan, and it was as he had said. The stress of events had been far too heavy for her; she lay on the floor of the short passage, her eyes closed, her breathing deep and hard.

'Doctor,' I told him, 'it's luckier than I can say having bumped into you like this. The poor woman's's all in — she's been viciously lashed by a hulking swine.'

He raised horrified hands. 'Tell me later. Now you must bring her into this back room here, and I will examine her injuries. I am afraid I can't lift her myself. I'm not as young as I once was.'

I nodded and picked Joan up again; he led the way into a neatly furnished room illuminated by a large window at about head level. He pointed towards the couch, then busied himself with ointment and bandages. Finally he turned to me and said: 'Where are the wounds?'

'She's badly lacerated on the back, Doctor,' I told him. I turned Joan on her face and slid down her hastily donned white dress from her shoulders. This was no time for false modesty. The angry welts stood out, crusted with drying blood, and Doctor Harmer shook his head.

'This is terrible. I must clean them. Meanwhile, you can pour yourself a glass of brandy, Mr. Maynard. You'll find it in the small cabinet in that corner.'

I poured the drink, and sat watching as he tended Joan's wounds. They were, of course, only superficial, but bad enough, and likely to be very painful when she came round. Harmer worked silently and skilfully, first cleansing, then treating and dressing the lacerations. At last he stood up, drew Joan's dress back into place, and washed his hands, saying: 'Now, Mr. Maynard, if you'll give her a sip of brandy she'll be with us in no time.'

I did so, and watched her eyelids flutter open. She gazed round in surprise, then relief. 'We — we got away, Colin?'

'Thanks to the doctor, here. He also dressed your wounds.'

She looked bewildered. 'Doctor?'

'Yes, a friend of mine — I met him on board the ship. We chose his doorway to hide in, thank God. But for that . . . '

Harmer came over, smiling, and I said: 'Miss Kennett — Doctor Harmer.'

She took his hand. 'You saved us, Doctor? How can we ever repay you?'

He waved away her thanks and gave her more brandy. 'I don't want repayment. I'm glad I was able to help you. How did it all happen?'

She shook her head hopelessly. 'I'm an artist — I work for an English magazine. They wanted some sketches of Egypt and I was sent for them. I was working in the native quarter, which is by far the most picturesque portion of the town, when I was suddenly grabbed and taken through an archway into another building. Then I was stripped, and asked by an Arab what I was doing there. I told him I'd been sketching, but he didn't seem to believe that. He sent for a large brute of a man, and ordered him to — to whip me . . . I think perhaps Colin can tell the rest better.'

I explained my part in the affair, and when I had finished the doctor shook his head. 'I can't understand it. There wouldn't seem to be any point in the whipping at all. Are you sure the Arab didn't directly *accuse* you of something?'

She thought a minute, then said: 'He did say he had reason to believe I'd been listening to the conversation in the eating house. But what difference would that make?'

'It might make a lot of difference,' said Harmer, 'depending on what the conversation was about. Do you remember?'

'Not a syllable. There was so much jabbering going on, and I was sketching, so I didn't catch any of it.'

'A pity,' said Harmer. 'It may have been important. What do you mean to do now

— report to the authorities?'

'No — no, I won't report it,' she said. 'It would be rather embarrassing. You see, I was warned not to venture far into the native quarters.'

'I think you're very foolish,' said Harmer, shaking his head.

'I have a theory that this is all the work of those damned Sons of the Sphinx,' I chimed in. 'I don't know why I should think that, but I do.' The thought of the children at play came back to my mind, and I repeated it to the doctor.

He inclined his head gravely. 'Yes, since I was last here the power of the organization has grown by leaps and bounds. I still do not know what their object is, but certainly there's something wrong with the town. The natives are uneasy — the whole place seems to be brooding, waiting . . . for what, I have no idea. I am beginning to think the organization has sown the seeds of revolt here!'

'With things in their present troubled condition that wouldn't be so hard,' I admitted. 'You think they are a terrorist society?'

'I'm not sure. They must be after *something*. I have the feeling that everyone in the native quarter knows all about them, but they simply won't talk. Frankly, I'd advise you and your friends to return to Cairo until this trouble is over — if there is to be any trouble. You can only run your heads into danger if you stay here, and the Sons of the Sphinx have a score to settle with you.'

'That's up to Maurice,' I said. 'And I think I know what his answer will be — no.'

We talked of this and that for a time, and finally the doctor announced that the coast would presumably be clear by now. It was, and after we had shaken hands with him we ventured out into the street, and on his advice went at once to the busier part of the town to pick up Trix and Bob. They were still at the café, waiting, and greeted our arrival with considerable joy — especially that of Joan. I told them the story and they were shocked. While they finished their drinks I took Joan aside.

'Joan,' I told her, 'you can't possibly

stay here, now. They intend to do you some harm, that's clear. Why not come back with me?'

'That's sweet of you, Colin, but honestly I can . . . '

'Don't you say you can look after yourself,' I warned her sternly. 'Not after what happened today.' She laughed. I went on, persuasively: 'We'd all be glad to have you along, I know. Plenty of room for you, and if you're bent on doing these sketches, you'll be able to sketch the Pyramid of Khufu — we leave for there tomorrow.'

'Of course,' she said thoughtfully. 'The Pyramid of Khufu!'

'It'll make a fine subject,' I said eagerly. 'Being off the regular pyramid belt, I don't suppose many sketches and photographs have been made of it.'

'Yes, it *will* be interesting,' she agreed. 'They say it's similar to the Pyramid of Djoser at Saqqara — the Step Pyramid. One or two people hold it as being the first pyramid built — the choice seems to lie between that one, and that of Djoser. I *should* rather like to draw it.'

'Then you'll come along?' I asked eagerly.

'You're sure my presence won't annoy or hinder you all?'

'On the contrary — it'll cheer us up. That's settled then. From now on you are through looking after yourself. You've got yourself a bodyguard. And,' I went on, 'I couldn't think of anybody I'd like to guard more!'

★ ★ ★

I hadn't expected Maurice to raise any objection to Joan's company, but I certainly hadn't expected him to hail her with as much cordiality as he did. I believe, if he had had a red carpet, he would have laid it down for her!

However, his object became clear to me immediately after supper that same night. He buttonholed me and drew me aside, his eyes never leaving the charming profile of the girl as she sat at the table talking pleasantly with Professor Grimm. He said: 'Colin, you're a genius!'

'I am? Why?' I asked, unused to such flattery.

'She's perfect,' he went on ecstatically. 'Just the type for the part. All we have to do now is to persuade her to take Sandra's place.'

'Here, wait a minute,' I said hastily. 'I didn't bring her along as our leading lady. What makes you think she can act?'

'A born actress,' he said. 'I can spot 'em a mile off. She's a natural.'

'I wouldn't be surprised if you were right,' I said, nodding. 'But that doesn't say she'd *want* the part. Besides, even if she did, she's got blonde hair. How about that?'

'Sandra was going to wear a wig,' he told me. 'I dare say it would fit her. Miss Black could make a few alterations if they were needed.'

'Well, you can ask her if you like,' I said dubiously.

He kneaded my arm coaxingly. 'No, *you* ask her, Colin. You rescued her from God knows what, and she seems to be pretty fond of you — why, I can't think, but there it is. You will?'

I sighed and agreed. I always did find it hard to refuse Maurice anything. He's that kind of a man.

'Look here, Joan,' I said, later still, as we stood at the edge of the desert under a large brilliant moon. 'I've been thinking . . . '

She gave my arm a squeeze and smiled at me. 'Thinking what?'

'Oh, about Maurice, and how broken up he is. You see, Sandra, the leading lady, and the most important person in the cast, walked out on him at Giza. Now we're stuck without anyone to play the lead, and if he alters the script he's sure to make a botch of it. Besides, what use is a film like this without a beautiful woman in it?'

She remained silent. Encouraged, I rushed on. 'I thought that since you're going along with us, perhaps you wouldn't mind taking on the title role of the film — *Flame of the Pyramids*. Maurice says you're just right for it, and . . . '

'So you and Maurice cooked this up between you, did you?' she said, looking at the sand.

'Yes, I suppose we did. It'd be a full-time job, mind, and you'd have to sandwich your sketches in between takes.

You'd get Sandra's salary, I expect, and that isn't to be sneezed at.'

'It isn't the salary I want,' she said. 'If you think I could manage the part, I'd be only too willing to do it. You and Maurice have been so kind to me — I feel safer here with you, I admit that now. Yes, if you really do want me to do it, I accept.'

I gripped her hand and she suddenly looked up into my eyes. She said softly: 'I hated parting from you on the ship, Colin. I didn't think that little flirtation we had could matter, but it did. Now I'm with you, and staying with you, you may as well know I didn't mean any of the things I said in that eating place today. I'd never wanted anyone beside me as I wanted you to stay then. When you walked out I could have screamed.'

'Then why — why did you practically force me to leave?'

She gazed thoughtfully at a clump of palm trees for a moment before replying. 'I can trust you to hold what I am going to tell you as a confidence, can't I? I shouldn't really be telling you, but after all, you saved me from . . . possibly death.

'My real name is Joan Hayes, not Kennett. I am not an artist and I do not work for any magazine. That is a blind. I am number twenty-three, British Secret Service. Some time ago rumours reached official ears that a band of cut-throats calling themselves the Sons of the Sphinx planned to start a revolution of the native classes here. The date chosen was the tenth of this month, and it's now the *seventh!* How and what they planned to do we couldn't discover — and so I was sent out to Saqqara.

'We knew that their hold was strong in that district; and we also knew members were in the habit of visiting the eating house you saw me in. I went there today, ostensibly as an artist, but actually to see what I could hear. They must have seen me listening to the talk that was going on, and you know what happened then. They tried to find out if I really was an artist, and if not what I was doing there at all. Thanks to you they didn't succeed. But a few more lashes and I never could have held out.

'I didn't hear a great deal in that café

— but I did hear one word repeated several times. That was Tarfa. And another word was a close runner-up — Khufu. What exactly is going to take place at Tarfa, and at the Pyramid of Khufu, I couldn't find out; but when you suggested my going along with you, I realized what a fine opportunity it would be to investigate the pyramid. Alone, they'd almost certainly kill me; but with a party, it won't be as easy for them.'

'It'll be damned awkward,' I told her, having recovered from my first surprise. 'Because since these murders took place, we all move about armed. So you're *really* a secret service agent?' She nodded, and I said: 'And that was how you managed to get off the boat at Alexandria?'

'That was it. Bribery didn't enter into it. I told the official not to attract any attention to my departure. That was probably why he swore to you that I hadn't left the ship. I hope you weren't too annoyed?'

'I was at the time,' I told her. 'I didn't want you to leave like that without even a goodbye. That's why I was cut up about the way you skipped the ship.'

'I felt the same way,' she admitted. 'But what could I do? I didn't know you half as well then; I couldn't possibly have put my trust in you.'

'Oh, I don't know so much about that — I always kidded myself I had an honest face.'

'You've got a wonderful face,' she said with a smile, 'but it definitely isn't what you would call honest. Honest faces, I think, are so plain and uninteresting. Like round moons. Don't you agree?'

'I suppose they are in a way,' I said. 'I've often found that an utterly unscrupulous person can be truly beautiful.'

'You've met an unscrupulous woman?'

'Lots of times. Aren't all women unscrupulous?'

She laughed. 'I suppose they are — particularly when it comes to men. But we mustn't generalize. We're on a thorny subject!'

We dropped the matter and took in the beauty of the night. It had its effect on us both, and for some time after that our lips were too busy for idle conversation . . .

7

The Pyramid of Khufu

We made an early start the following day; the equipment, our two cameramen, Joan, Miss Black, Maurice, the professor, Strong and myself travelling in a large specially constructed motor truck, and the fellah and 'Joe,' our dragoman, riding mules and carrying some of our provisions.

The first part of our journey was easy, since we were travelling across hard stretches of sand and limestone; we took a slightly circular route, pausing for a time to take a look at the Statue of Rameses the Second, and the ruined — though still majestic — city of Memphis, which many thousands of years ago had been the capital of Egypt, then inhabited by a mighty and learned people.

After this our route led past the pyramids and the Tombs of Dahshur, and since there was little of interest to us here, we carried straight on, Maurice being a little impatient for his first sight of Khufu. We had come so far, and so much depended upon the pyramid, that each one of us could not help feeling mounting excitement and eagerness as Professor Grimm notified us that we were drawing nearer. And we arrived before the full fierce heat of midday began to beat down upon us.

The pyramid lay in a shallow valley of sandstone covered by a layer of gritty sand about a foot deep. As we breasted the rise and gazed down upon it, no one spoke for minutes. Then Maurice said: 'It's perfect — perfect!'

The truck purred to life again and lurched down into the centre of the valley; and as we progressed, the Pyramid loomed ever larger and we could see it in more detail. Like that at Saqqara, it was a step pyramid. It was smaller, but in a quite remarkable state of preservation. There were eight tiers or steps of stone leading up to a flat top about fifty feet square. In the centre of this top was an excavation in the shape of a square, roofless room, and leading from this into passages which ran directly into the heart of the pyramid were several oblong openings. The exterior was rough, of course, and always had been, for at the time it had been built, outer polished casing had not been thought of by the masons. But as Maurice had said, it was ideal for our purpose; and being so far from the usual pyramid belt there was not a soul to be seen about the place.

Perhaps by 'step pyramid' I do not make the shape of the thing quite clear. In that case, imagine a square wedding cake built up in six tiers, one above the other, with a flat top, and there you have the principle of the structure as nearly as I can define it; each higher tier or terrace becoming smaller than the one below it, both in height and length.

Our fellah unloaded our tents and equipment and pitched camp in a spot they knew would afford the most protection, should we catch the edge of a desert sandstorm. By four o'clock we were ready to inspect the pyramid; and Joan, the cameramen, Maurice, Grimm and myself climbed to the summit of the pyramid with feelings of great excitement. Grimm gave us a brief résumé of the history of the pyramid as we stood in the top excavation.

'Khufu's time cannot be correctly defined,' he informed us. 'Apparently he was either not a very important king, or the records had not then been undertaken completely. The hieroglyphs and the portraits on the pyramid walls give us no idea of the probable date of his rule, although we estimate it at 1600 B.C. Inside the royal chamber there are stucco relief wall portraits of the pharaoh in various everyday poses, and from the story these tell we gather that he was an able ruler, and a just one.

'The mummy, when found, was practically nothing but dust, for at that time the system of mummifying was still, at times, imperfect; and the ravages of Arabs in the past had destroyed whatever was left of Khufu. The same Arabs had plundered the pyramid, leaving only an occasional article too large to carry away with them. These articles — a number of basalt statues and one or two wooden carvings of gods — are now in Cairo Museum. Of course, as you know, for the purpose of the film the government have loaned us a wooden inner sarcophagus. The outer case, in this instance, we were unable to remove, for it is carved from a solid block of granite, and embedded in the floor of the burial chamber.

'The whole pyramid is a maze of tunnels, and we must be very cautious, for to prevent vandals getting at the dead pharaoh there are many deep pits into which the unwary might fall and seriously injure themselves. It is believed that Khufu's queen was buried here, for some of the hieroglyphs contain references to the queen's chamber, which invariably lies below the king's; be that as it may, an extensive expedition failed to discover any trace of this second chamber. There is not, as usual, a connecting tunnel from the king's chamber to the queen's. Now, if we are going straight to the burial chamber we take this right-hand tunnel mouth. Follow me and keep your torches going.'

We listened enthralled, for the professor had had much lecturing experience, and spoke well and briefly. Reading his words in lifeless print might seem boring enough; but to stand above the spot where years before Christ was born a great ruler had been laid to rest, conveyed a thrill which was indescribable. The mere idea that thousands of hands had fashioned that pyramid when the world was incredibly young caused a strange silence to fall upon us, even upon the voluble Trix.

We traversed a gloomy passage leading downwards into the bowels of the pyramid. This ran for forty feet without a break in the monotony of the grey stone about us; but suddenly we burst out into a small chamber, and we stood in wonder as our torches picked out the still-bright colours of the wall murals of King Khufu at work and play.

No words of mine are apt enough to describe that scene; I will leave it to your imagination mainly, merely referring to the roof of the room, which was painted black and studded with painted stars; and the angular, life-size figures of the king on his throne, on his barge on the Nile, and prostrating himself before Isis.

Grimm said in a subdued voice: 'This chamber contained magic figures carved in wood, and meant to serve the dead pharaoh in his journey through the Other World. Much of the stuff had been pilfered, and what remained had been badly chipped and broken; but we found a marching panther, the head of a cow, and an open left hand. It is probable there was a great deal more which the looters took. There's another short passage here, and then we reach the ante-chamber.'

The ante-chamber, smaller but nonetheless gloriously decorated, occupied us for some time while we studied the portraits on the walls. Then at last the professor led us into an inner chamber greater than either of the other two, and pointed to a massive stone upon which stood the granite sarcophagus. We looked down into the now-deserted resting place, and we could picture the calm majesty of the dead, mummified pharaoh lying in state, with a single scarab on his chest to ward off evil.

Maurice said: 'Think you can get the

lighting effects here, Trix?'

Trix nodded. 'Sure. We brought along the right stuff, chief. When do you figure on making a start?'

Maurice scratched his head. 'Suppose we fix up the first set right now? I want to get the shot of the mummy coming to life — that's important, and we can cut it into the takes afterwards.'

'That will mean bringing the sarcophagus along?' said Grimm. 'And the papier-mâché mummy?'

'Sure. The way we'll do it will be like this: we'll get the shot of Rodney descending into the queen's chamber — '

'*King's* chamber,' corrected Grimm.

'It's a *queen's* chamber in the screenplay,' Maurice said.

'Dear me,' Grimm sighed. 'In that case I'm afraid the paintings on the walls won't be authentic.'

'That's okay,' Maurice said, smiling. 'We aren't catering for a lot of people who know their Egypt. The idea of a mummy coming to life isn't authentic either, but the audience'll lap it up! Now we get the shot of Rodney entering the

pyramid and finding the queen's chamber
— Trix will have his lighting fixed ready
down here. The dummy mummy will be
laid inside the wooden sarcophagus and
then placed into the granite one, here.
We'll fit the false lid we brought along for
the top of this granite coffin, and take a
shot of Rodney using a hammer and
chisel on it, then a crowbar.

'He gets the lid off, and stares down at
the mummy inside. Then we cut, bandage
Miss Kennett up like the false mummy,
and she gets into the sarcophagus and
moves — but we'll fix that when we get to
it. Right — now let's fix the lighting and
the set. Get those fellah to bring the
sarcophagus along with the paper mummy
in it. Let's move.'

We all returned to the outside, and Grimm
got busy directing the removal of the painted
sarcophagus containing the fake mummy
into the tomb. Trix arranged his lighting,
and then there was a call for Miss Black,
the wardrobe mistress. But Miss Black
was not to be found: Joe, the dragoman,
informed us that she had followed us into
the pyramid after arranging her costumes,

and had not returned as yet.

Professor Grimm looked anxious. 'The woman must have lost herself in the passages. I'd better get along and start looking for her.'

'Is there any danger?' asked Joan. 'Hadn't we better help?'

'No, no. It's all right as long as she keeps her torch on. You people had better start making your picture — there isn't much daylight left now, and you need the scene where your Egyptologist climbs up the pyramid. Go ahead.'

Grimm disappeared into the pyramid again, and we all gathered round to watch the first take. Maurice wasn't being particular about this; he was counting on the strangeness and authenticity of the setting to put the movie over.

Rodney got in position, and Maurice said: 'All right, *shoot*.'

The cameras started to turn as Rodney began to climb. Trix took the rear shots, and Bob Lieberman took shots from the top of the pyramid of Strong's eager face as he ascended.

Halfway up Trix cut and hurried his

camera along to the flat pyramid top, ready for the shot of Rodney approaching the tunnel mouth. It was difficult work with only two cameras, and meant a lot of dashing about, but Trix was quite adequate to the task. The scene went on, Bob taking shots of Rodney walking carefully down the tunnel from behind, and Trix, camera now set up at the entrance to the king's chamber, covering the minutes which brought Rodney into the burial place itself.

Here there was a cut while cameras were set up beside the sarcophagus, and at the side of the wall, to get a take of Rodney's face when the mummy came to light.

The wooden lid clattered off, and sounded like nothing less than granite — but that didn't matter. Sounds would be dubbed into the track back in the studios. He worked on the lid of the wooden sarcophagus, then; this too was pried off, and the camera Trix was handling swivelled for a close-up of the mummy.

And the mummy *groaned!*

Never have I seen such a look of sheer

horror on anyone's features as that on Rodney's at that moment. Maurice saw it too, and yelled to Lieberman: 'Keep taking — *get his face!*'

Bob kept taking, grimly, until Rodney staggered back with a horrified cry.

Maurice shouted: 'Cut.'

We all crowded round the mummy, and Joan shivered. 'It — it isn't the same! It isn't the *fake* mummy!'

I think I realized then what must have taken place. I said to Maurice, soberly: 'Give me a hand to get it out.'

We caught the mummy under the arm-pits and raised it. And we saw the long, sharp knife, sticking into its back . . .

We saw more — we saw the blood oozing about the hilt, the bandages stained red — and beneath it, the papier-mâché imitation, now denuded of its wrappings!

Frantically Maurice ripped the bandages from the mummy's face. The glazed eyes and panic-stricken features of Miss Black came into view . . .

★   ★   ★

Miss Black was still alive, but unconscious, when we got her out onto the flat pyramid top. She didn't speak, and died a few minutes later.

It was ten minutes after her death that Professor Grimm emerged from the tunnels with the words: 'I can't find a trace of her anywhere — I — *Good God!*'

He had seen the body, and the following ten minutes were spent in explanations. Then he said grimly: 'There's only one thing we can do now — we must search the pyramid from top to bottom. She must have been attacked in there, stabbed, wrapped in the bindings of the fake mummy, and laid in the sarcophagus. Which means that somewhere in those passages there's a murderer — or murderers.'

Maurice agreed instantly, although I saw him look at Grimm rather strangely. And the same thought crossed my mind — Grimm *could* have done it! Certainly he was the only member of our party who had not been in sight when the murder had taken place. Could he have seized the opportunity to kill Miss Black?

Had he some reason himself for wishing to drive us away?

However, Maurice had the small arms brought out, and gave us each a revolver. We split up into parties of two: Maurice and Rodney Strong — who didn't look very strong at the moment; Trix and Bob Lieberman; and Grimm and Yusef, the dragoman. The rest of the fellah refused to risk their necks in those passages, and I can't say I really blamed them.

Joan elected to accompany me, and we chose a tunnel mouth to the left. Before we all started out, Grimm again warned us not to take chances and to keep torches going.

I hadn't imagined that the pyramid could contain as many passages, leading precisely nowhere, as it did. They branched and twisted at inconceivable angles, doubling back on themselves like a maze, and before we had been searching half an hour we were hopelessly lost. Once we heard footsteps echoing nearby, but a shout elicited no response, and we trudged on.

Joan said: 'I expect it'll be almost dark

113

outside now. Do you think we ought to go back? We haven't found anything, have we?'

'I think it's a damned good idea,' I told her. 'But do you know which way *is* back?'

She stared at me. 'Don't you?'

'I haven't the faintest. We've turned and twisted so many times I don't know if we're going or coming. We're lost.'

'Oh, Colin!'

I patted her shoulder. 'Don't worry, honey. We're bound to get someplace sometime. We'll just keep going, and chance to luck. We can't get lost for any length of time in a place this small.'

'I'm not so sure, Colin,' she said worriedly. 'These passages were built for the purpose of throwing any robbers into confusion. I expect more than one found them effective.'

I laughed uneasily. 'Nonsense. We're sure to come out some time. A person couldn't get so hopelessly lost that he died from starvation . . . '

'Couldn't he, Colin?' she said slowly, and following her gaze I jumped. We had turned into a blank tunnel, and at the far end, its bony hands outstretched as if clawing the wall, lay a skeleton without a shred of flesh on it. I shuddered, and hastily steered a fresh course. We tramped on, spirits getting lower and lower.

I have been in mazes all over the world, but never have I found one as cleverly constructed as was that of the Pyramid of Khufu. Again and again we found ourselves back at that skeleton; it haunted us, and made us realize that before he had died, the man who lay there had probably been in the same plight as ourselves. We just couldn't seem to break away from that particular section of the tomb, no matter which way we turned.

With unfailing regularity, every ten minutes or so, up would pop that gruesome relic; and though I did my best to cheer Joan up, I was beginning to think we ourselves might wind up like that.

Then, at last, half an hour passed without us seeing the pile of human bones again. And considerably cheered up, although tired and aching, we pressed on with renewed hope. Five more minutes, and at the top of a long gloomy tunnel, we saw a flicker of fading daylight! Joan gave a little thankful gasp, and hurried forward eagerly.

The next minute she had *vanished*, and only a quivering scream in the air remained to show she had been there at all!

8

The Queen's Chamber

For almost a minute I was too stunned to do anything; then I played my torch-beam over the ground before me, and saw the three-foot square, gaping black pit into which Joan had fallen. Cold fear held me motionless — I could picture her shattered body far below, impaled on God knew what horrible devices — but finally I snapped my tension and knelt by the pit side, staring down.

The pit was about fifteen feet deep; and on the sandy floor sat Joan, rubbing her head dazedly. I was overjoyed, and called: 'Hello — Joan — Joan, are you hurt?'

'No, thank goodness,' she replied, glancing up, 'but there's *another tunnel* leading off this pit . . . '

'There is?'

'Yes, a very low one — and the sand here looks as though it's recently been disturbed. Can you get down, Colin?'

'I'll have a shot.'

I knelt, and clenching my torch between my teeth, lowered myself until I hung from my fingertips. I let go, and the drop of nine feet made me reel backwards, but Joan's hands stopped me from falling. I recovered and shone the torch about.

In the left side of the pit was a low tunnel, hardly more than four feet high. I flashed the light along it, but it ran as far as the torch beam would penetrate, and revealed nothing.

As Joan had said, there were footprints running into it; and they were prints which had not been made by any bare foot, or by a native shoe or sandal! They were imprints of nailed, European shoes!

I gripped Joan's hand and said: 'I'm going along there. It looks as if we're onto something.'

She nodded. 'I'm coming with you. It's my job, remember!'

I didn't attempt to dissuade her; actually I was glad of her company. I took the lead, and bent low we pressed forward into the tunnel. I don't know why, but every step of that journey I had the continual fear of being struck down; in fancy I seemed to feel the crash of a club upon my bent head. It was a terrible sensation; a sensation of being helpless and doomed. But we reached the end of the tunnel without mishap, and came to a strong stone door which stood slightly open.

Beyond this was yet another passage, but this was high enough for us to stand upright, and was quite wide. Hieroglyphs now began to appear on the walls, and occasional paintings portraying a lady with very thin features in various poses. We arrived at an open chamber, and here were treasures indeed: carvings of gods, hawks, fishes, and animals; ancient tables and chairs loaded with delicately worked jewellery; bowls of spices, tightly sealed against the action of the air.

I knew at once we had found the hitherto missing queen's chamber!

And what lay beyond? Should we find the mummy of the queen?

The further door opened to my touch;

and this time I could hardly believe my eyes!

The sarcophagus was there — doubtless with its mummy still inside. So were the four jars near it, containing the liver, heart and other organs of her embalmed body. And stacked against the walls, piled high, were modern rifles, machine guns, boxes of ammunition and explosives!

More than this — on closer inspection, I discovered a pile of army uniforms in new condition. What did this mean? What *could* it mean?

One thing was certain — these guns weren't any part of the treasures buried with Queen who-ever-she-was.

Joan had gripped my arm, her eyes shining. She said: 'This is what I wanted to know — what I *came* for. It's clear this is the storeroom of the Sons of the Sphinx. I must get the information back to Cairo headquarters at once.'

'Look here,' I said, crossing the room and picking up a few canvas bags from the lid of the sarcophagus. '*Food!* Someone is down here. Or has been.'

And both of us realized the peril we

stood in. Whoever was hiding out here might be aware that we were in the chamber. He could be watching from any one of the three tunnels that led off the chamber. He could be . . .

Like a darting lance of fire in the torch-gleam, a long, thin knife whined past my head and clattered against the sarcophagus. Even before it had reached the floor I had switched off my torch, and forcing Joan behind the stone slab, had gone to my knees.

'We've got to get out of here,' I whispered. 'God knows where he is, or how many we're facing. We'll have to chance one of the tunnels.'

She whispered assent, and I got out my revolver. I stood up. 'I'm making for the right-hand tunnel,' I said. 'You follow me as soon as I switch on the torch.'

I crossed silently in darkness, until I was within about two feet of the wall. Then I flipped the switch and dashed into the mouth of the tunnel nearest me, holding my gun ready.

The tunnel was empty. Not a sound disturbed the stillness. I heard Joan's running feet, and then she had joined me.

'Now quickly,' I panted. 'This *must* lead somewhere. We'd better put on the pace. You come in front of me and take the torch; if we're followed I'll deal with whoever comes after us.'

If I peered over my shoulder once during that run for life, I peered a hundred times. There was no knowing which moment would see a whizzing knife flying into my back. But nothing happened. Apparently any pursuers we had, had been fooled by our sudden rush. At long last we saw the end of the tunnel in sight ahead. Another few seconds and we were out — in the desert!

The tunnel had finished in the base of a small hill of sandstone. Before the tunnel mouth stood a huge drift of sand, which acted as useful camouflage for the entrance. Joan and I climbed up this and I soon had my bearings. The sandstone rise comprised the west side of the valley in which lay the pyramid. Beyond the rise we would find the truck and our friends again, I hoped.

Sure enough, we were not disappointed.

Breasting the sandstone, we gazed down on top of the pyramid. We could see a little knot of figures grouped together in the excavation. We hurried down the slope, and when we were halfway there they saw us, waved, and started climbing down from the pyramid top.

The first thing I thought of was having a guard placed on the entrance to the tunnel mouth. Two of the fellah were detailed off; armed with rifles they were told to watch, and if anyone tried to leave that tunnel to fire to kill.

Then we held a council of war about the motor truck. 'Whoever's done the killing is in there,' I said, pointing to the pyramid. 'It would be hopeless to try to find them; if we all went inside they'd probably be able to pick us off one by one.'

'Then what do you suggest?' asked Maurice.

'I can only see one way,' I told him. 'Everyone must be armed, then you must set a guard round the place. Every tunnel mouth on the top excavation must be watched. No exit must be neglected.'

'But we can't watch forever,' protested Bob Lieberman.

'You won't need to — before long we'll have troops from Cairo down here and they can deal with all this.'

'I'm going into Cairo to report,' Joan said. 'I'll stop off at Saqqara and do what I can there first to get things moving.'

'And I'm going along with you,' I told her. 'It isn't safe for you to chance it alone. You stand a risk of bumping into all kinds of danger between here and Saqqara.'

'But hadn't two men better go?' protested Maurice. 'I mean Miss Kennett would be safer here, wouldn't she?'

'There's something you ought to know about Joan,' I said. 'Is it all right to tell them?'

'I think so — it can't do any harm now, can it?'

'Joan is a British agent,' I told them, smiling at the blank looks on their faces. 'She'll be able to get things moving more quickly than we would. Meanwhile you must watch that pyramid. Whatever is scheduled to happen is not scheduled to happen until the tenth, as far as we know. We'll be back before then with help.'

Maurice said: 'In that case you'd better take the truck. And good luck, Colin — and you, Joan. It *is* still Joan, yes?'

She nodded; we all shook hands, and without waiting to see the guard posted, we climbed in the truck, and I drove off. I took a compass bearing, set the nose of the truck in the direction of Saqqara and the Nile, and coaxed every ounce of power from the heavy engines. We had covered perhaps two miles when Joan said: 'Colin — look!'

I looked, and on a hillock of sand, far to the right, I saw an Arab horseman. The horse and rider were stationary; his hand was to his eyes, and he was outlined against the moonlight, which made the desert almost as plain as daylight. The next second he had vanished, leaving me wondering if he had been only a mirage.

'Some wandering tribesman,' I said, but Joan shook her head and replied:

'I'm worried — he seemed to be looking directly at us.'

And suddenly the desert was alive with

riders and horses! From every direction they rose to view, and spurring their horses wildly, rode in, converging on our truck. I seized a rifle from the rear seat and Joan did likewise. Then I stopped the truck and we waited, both of us feeling that this was the end.

'It's been great knowing you, Joan,' I told her. 'And it's too bad this had to happen.'

'And I've loved knowing you,' she whispered. I felt her lips brush my cheek lightly; then we were firing from each window at the Arabs who were now circling round us.

There were no cries; no bloodthirsty howls from these men. They rode in silence, like warriors who had been well trained. They didn't attempt to use the rifles they bore on us, and in spite of the few we picked off, they evinced no panic, just kept circling and circling monotonously.

My hammer clicked on an empty chamber. 'I'm out of ammunition,' I said, 'and the rest is in the *back* of the truck. Now what?'

Joan fired her last shot. 'There's nothing else to be done, then. We'll just have to be taken.'

The Arab horsemen had realized our position and were closing in. A fine strapping young rider reined in his mount by the side of our truck and grated: 'You are to come with us, Effendi. Do not give us any more trouble. Start up your motor.'

Surrounded by the weird mixture of Bedouins, Tuareg and other tribes, we drove off, taking a route opposite to that of Saqqara. The drive lasted half an hour; and then on the horizon a clump of palms loomed up.

'An oasis,' breathed Joan.

I called to the man who was riding alongside. 'Where are we going?'

'That you will find out,' he sneered. 'As you will find out it is unwise to meddle with the Sons of the Sphinx.'

'You are members of the Sons of the Sphinx?' I asked him, and he nodded his burnoosed head in assent. I continued: 'But we know nothing of you. We are two innocent travellers.'

He roared with laughter at this, then snarled: 'It is of no use to lie. Ever since you arrived at the pyramid you have been watched. You did not see us, but we saw you. And there is one of our number within the pyramid himself. He went there when he learned that your expedition had started out for Khufu, and tonight he signalled us from the tunnel mouth to say that you had discovered the queen's chamber, and that none of you must be allowed to leave the pyramid.'

'I see,' I said. 'You intend to kill us then?'

'Perhaps, later. But first we must take you to our beloved ruler. She who is in supreme command of us. She will decide what we shall do to you two.'

'You are led by a — woman?' I asked, surprised.

'Ay. A queen, who will soon sit upon the throne of Egypt and bring to our country prosperity.'

I sank back behind the wheel again and looked at Joan. 'You heard?'

'Yes — so when they have started their revolution they plan to place a woman on

Egypt's throne. Surely they must realize they can't get away with it? A bunch of natives can't oppose the British army. It's fantastic.'

'I don't know. Think of all the natives there are in Egypt. Think of what would happen if they gained control of the Suez Canal and Port Said. Certainly they would be brought to heel in the end, but what a terrible amount of bloodshed there would be. All the government troops would be butchered by the native population.'

'I admit that — but the majority of the people know the British rule has been the most beneficial form of government they have ever enjoyed. How could these fanatical few convince the people that a revolt against authority could benefit them?'

'I'd give a lot to know that. I believe they have some scheme — something to do with Khufu and Tarfa, and probably with the army uniforms they have hidden in the pyramid. But exactly how they plan to use them, I'm completely at a loss.'

We had drawn near to an Arab

encampment about fifty yards from the small oasis. Shabby tents were clustered together on the sand, and Arab women were at work over the fires, tending the cooking pots. To me it seemed there were three or four nomadic tribes gathered for some purpose — and in the middle of the other tents stood one large affair, of glorious silk!

We were dragged from the truck and tied hand and foot. Then we were roughly tossed aside, being told that the queen would see us after she had 'supped.'

There was nothing to do but lay there and speculate, gibed at by some Arab women, and kicked by their passing menfolk. It was some time before we were dragged to our feet and hoisted towards the silken tent.

They held us upright before the entrance, while one of our captors went within. We clearly heard a woman's voice say: 'I will see them now, Abras.'

Then we were forced roughly into the tent, and flung on the floor in front of a gorgeous silken divan. I raised my eyes from the dirt beneath me and gasped at what I saw. The woman seated upon the divan was statuesquely graceful. She sat still and impassive, gazing down at us from mysterious almond-shaped eyes. Her skin was fairer than that of the average Egyptian, and her perfect figure was gowned in an expensive evening dress of the latest design. This, then was their ruler!

'Felicitations, O Queen,' I said, and she stared at me, then waved an imperious hand to her henchmen, who left the tent.

'Are you endeavouring to be sarcastic, Mr. Maynard?' she asked in flawless English.

'Why not?' I demanded. 'Since we are about to die anyway, why should I not drag what little consolation I can out of irony?'

She smiled. 'I thought you weren't serious. So you think because you are near to death you can afford to mock me? Have a care, Mr. Maynard. That death can be easy — or I can have it made very, very unpleasant!'

I knew by her eyes it was no joke. And I decided to curb my sarcasm for the time being. 'Who are you?' I asked.

'My name is Nilita Kolay, Mr. Maynard. Until recently I was quite a well-known figure in Egyptian society. But now, for my purpose, I am known as Cleopatra.'

'Cleopatra?' I echoed. 'Why?'

'It is a name by which the natives will be more easily swayed. To them I am a figure of mystery — they do not know whence I come, nor who I really am. Some believe that I am the reincarnation of the long-dead queen of Egypt, come to atone for the betrayal of her country, by delivering them from bondage. Yet others understand I can trace my lineage right back to Cleopatra herself.'

'That's nonsense,' I said. 'An impossibility.'

'To you, yes. And to me. But not to the poor superstitious fools whom I plan to make my subjects. They believe in me. Their belief has been fostered by years of hard spade work by picked men. On the tenth of this month they will cast off oppression and rise up against their masters. Once I hold the gateway to the east, it will be simple. Britain *will* accept the changed conditions as inevitable.'

'Will they?' I exclaimed. 'I doubt it.'

She leaned forward. 'But I am sure of it! There is a man who works for me — who placed this idea in my head, who *helped* to organize the Sons of the Sphinx. He believes Britain will bow out — and since he *is an Englishman*, he should know!'

9

The Plot for Revolt

'Why are you telling us all this?' Joan asked in a low voice.

'Why?' The woman shrugged. 'It can hardly matter what I tell you, since I will not give you any chance to repeat it. Besides, you have no idea what an ill-educated lot many of these Arabs and natives are. There are few among them with whom I can converse intelligently. It is quite a pleasure to be able to speak to educated people like yourselves.'

I had rolled over onto my side; I now said: 'We could talk much more comfortably if these bonds were loosened, and we were allowed to sit up.'

'But of course. How *stupid* of me,' she purred, with dripped sarcasm. She called sharply and two Arabs entered. She said: 'Remove the bonds from their ankles, and place them in those two seats.'

They bowed and did as directed. Soon we were seated more or less comfortably, facing the woman who desired to be queen of Egypt. The conversation Joan and I had once had about unscrupulous persons often being beautiful came back to my mind. Undoubtedly this woman was beautiful; her figure had a kind of feline grace, and although her olive features boasted one or two harsh lines, these added, rather than detracted, from her charm. No, charm is hardly the word I want to describe her peculiar quality; it was more fascination. She was like a beautifully poised snake, hissing softly, preparatory to the strike!

'It will interest you to know also,' she went on, 'that the members of your party who have so far been murdered owe their unfortunate ends entirely to this gentleman's ministrations. The really amusing part of it all is that he holds your complete confidence! Only yesterday he was the means of rescuing you and the lady from a nasty fate.'

'You mean . . . ' I stammered.

'Exactly. The man you know as Doctor

Harmer. He is my partner in this enterprise!'

I was too stunned to speak. Joan's eyes, too, were incredulous, and her features expressed disbelief.

'You find that hard to believe? I can't blame you. No one would suspect such a kind philanthropist as Doctor Harmer of being a scheming, plotting genius.'

'But — but what does *he* get out of it?' I demanded.

'Very little — except revenge. And revenge is all he wants — all he has lived for!'

'Revenge? Revenge on whom?' Joan gasped.

'Revenge on an entire nation,' the woman said with a smile. 'On England. Why do you suppose Dr. Harmer chose to work here, on the Nile, in all kinds of filthy conditions in the first place?'

'I had thought he was a good and kind man,' I told her, and she laughed and shook her head.

'No, no. He is very far from being a good and kind man. He cares nothing for the sufferings of the natives. The reason he came here in the first place was because he was running away.'

'Running away?'

'Exactly. From the scorn and derision of his own race! Here, in complete obscurity, he started tending the natives. He changed his name, for in England he was called Doctor Fortescue Crane. You may recall the case — he was struck from the rolls by the Supreme Medical Council for performing several illegal operations upon prominent society women, which the English law takes a very stern view of. He was quite fashionable with them, until a certain titled lady was left dangerously ill through his ministrations.

'The affair came to the ears of the police, and although the woman recovered, he served a term of imprisonment, and was then released to find that not only could he no longer practice, but that everyone held him in the greatest contempt. He is a sensitive man, and he pursued the only course open to him — he fled abroad, to Egypt, and under the name of Harmer, ministered to the natives, eking out a scanty living. I met him professionally some years ago, and we became good friends.

'From that meeting grew the Sons of the Sphinx, which he was instrumental in forming, from friends he had made amongst the natives. Our power grew ever greater, and finally our last scheme was born. Secretly we had been collecting arms for our men, and these are stored in dumps all over the country. Money was of little consequence — I have plenty — and with its aid we were able to get native workmen to make British uniforms for us.

'Then we read of your proposed expedition! Harmer was in England at the time, endeavouring to find out what he could about the positions and movements of troops in Egypt. He discovered the best time for our blow would be the tenth of this month. But your arrival upon the scene threatened to spoil all our work, and so he set out to frighten you off.

'His first attempt was a warning note — his second the murder of your cameraman in London. That failed, and he tried again on the ship coming over. This time he managed to scrape an acquaintance with you, and determined

138

your exact plans.

'The attack in the tomb at Giza was his work; but still you refused to be frightened off, and the position began to get serious. We had had reports of a young English woman snooping round Saqqara, particularly round the café, which is our headquarters there. Our members were given instructions to capture and question this person, and they did so — but your intervention, Mr. Maynard, ruined the plan. In your escape you came across Dr. Harmer's home, and he admitted you, not knowing who you were until it was too late; otherwise he would have left you to the natives.

'You informed him in the course of conversation that it was your intention to start for the pyramid the following day, and he knew that if you should discover anything there, all might well be lost. Accordingly he went there before you and installed himself in the queen's chamber, having decided to make one last attempt to frighten you off. Apparently this was unsuccessful, or you would not now be here.'

'We found the chamber,' I told her. 'And your arms and ammunition.'

'So Harmer signalled to the Sons of the Sphinx who were all round you. And thus, when you and the woman rode out, they had a good idea of where you were going.'

'Your whole plan is madness,' I told her grimly. 'You'll be wiped out! A handful of Arab natives can't prevail against a well-trained army. You must know that. Besides, how will you induce the fellah and natives to rise against their present rule? They are not blind, and even if your fantastic legend about Cleopatra has some influence on them, I hardly think it will be strong enough to foster revolt.'

She lit a cigarette. 'We are not relying on the legend alone. We know quite well that over three-quarters of the country appreciate, and wish to retain, British protection and their present system of government. But out fifth column have undermined their morale. They are like a keg of gunpowder, which the least spark will ignite. We plan to provide that spark — at Tarfa!'

She paused, drew thoughtfully at the smoke, and allowed it to trickle from her nostrils. 'It will be *very* simple,' she said. 'The tenth is particularly dark — there is no moon. Picked and trusted members of our band will ride into Tarfa, dressed in the uniform of soldiers. They will rape, loot, desecrate, and murder. They will leave the town a smouldering ruin. Others of our band will spread rebellion and mass hysteria. They will persuade the fellah that this is just the first of a hundred such incidents — that life along the Nile and in all Egypt is no longer safe. The spark will grow into a flame, and rifles will be distributed amongst the natives. They will take key positions. And we will gain control of artillery, strong points, and the Suez. All this will be done by means of those hundred uniforms hidden at Khufu — and your friends whom you left there, I fear, must be killed.'

Now that the whole devilish plan was made clear, I eyed the woman with scorn and loathing. That anyone so beautiful could be a party to such a massacre was hard to believe. But those little hard lines about the mouth and eyes told their story only too plainly; I knew this woman would stop at no fantastic scheme to reach for supreme power in Egypt.

'I recall just such another person as yourself — a man they called the Mad Dog of Europe,' I said. 'He, too, would stop at nothing to gain his ends — not even at the slaughter of his own countrymen. I have no need to tell you where that man is today.'

'Don't let us go into dramatics,' she said. 'He was a fool; he tried to overreach himself. I have no intention of making a bid for world supremacy — the Queen of Egypt will suit me perfectly.'

'Nevertheless,' I told her, 'your scheme will fail. Intelligent men and women will not be governed by an empty fake.'

'Intelligent men and women are in the minority here — any who dare to oppose my rule will be ruthlessly exterminated. As you two must be.'

'You may kill us,' I said slowly, 'but we will have the satisfaction of knowing that your own turn will come — that your bid cannot succeed; that your death, whether by trial or assassination, is inevitable. Your organization will be wiped from the face of Egypt by right-thinking men — just as that *other* was wiped from the face of Europe. Knowing that, I will die content.'

Her face, for the first time, betrayed malignancy. She came over, spat in my features, and snapped: 'I *will* succeed! And you will be here to witness my triumph! I will delay your deaths until such time as my rule is firmly established — and then you will die in the most unutterable torment the mind can devise. I will turn you over to the Arab women, and watch your squealing and howling. And you will die knowing that, had you not interfered, you would still have been safe in America.'

It was what I had been playing for — time. I knew her plan was futile, hopeless. I knew the revolution was doomed to failure before it even started. She herself could not see that, although probably Harmer realized it quite well. He was thinking only of causing trouble for the nation which had cast him out.

And if she were defeated, then we would be still alive — and safe.

She must have read my thoughts, for she smiled evilly. 'Should — by any chance — my attempt fail,' she said carefully, 'I will personally kill you before I myself am taken.' And then she called an order, and the two Arabs returned, bound us about the ankles again, and dragged us out.

We had been talking a long time; dawn was breaking over the oasis, and the red glow above the horizon hinted that soon the sun would be beating down upon the encampment. In accordance with the woman's orders, we were taken to a central square and tied flat, hands and legs outstretched, to four pegs driven into the ground. Any faint hope of escape I had held now vanished; escape was clearly impossible from such a position.

Neither of us talked; our spirits were too low. Today was the ninth.

The ninth!

And tomorrow, a horde of savage Arabs would ride upon Khufu, bringing death to the handful there who were waiting our return with reinforcements. I looked at Joan; her face was strained and taut, but her eyes were closed. Events had told their tale, and she had snatched the blessed security of sleep in her trouble.

My own eyes were heavy, but sleep would not come. I lay and watched the camp come to life, the women about their morning tasks, and the Arabs grooming their horses. A fierce itching racked my body, and I could feel the sand fleas digging into my soft flesh. The sun became a gigantic orb, burning down pitilessly upon my recumbent form. The skin of my face felt stretched and dry, and my tongue began to swell within my mouth. I would have given an arm for a spot of moisture to wet my lips with — but no one offered to give us a drink of any description.

I closed my eyes against the knife-like rays of the sun; but even then it scorched through my lids, making my eyeballs feel as if they were bursting from my skull — two white, inflamed masses of torture.

I glanced at Joan again and saw, thankfully, that she was *still* sleeping. And the terrible heat gradually brought sleep to me too. It was a disturbed and restless sleep; thoughts ran through my mind — not dreams.

I was back in the fifth grade at high school in Los Angeles. I saw the rows of desks, the sun streaming through the tall windows, and heard the sound of the bell calling us to lessons. But I wasn't going in to lessons — I was playing hooky! The scene shifted to the old swimming hole — I was stripped, plunging into the icy water, splashing, wriggling, spluttering with pleasure . . . Again that scene grew misty, and I was sitting in the corner drugstore, eating a double chocolate iced sundae. I could feel the great cool lumps of ice-cream sliding down my throat; I ate ravenously, ordering more and more . . .

I was in a slit trench in the desert . . . The last drops of water had been drained from my bottle, and we were *waiting* — waiting for these damned jack-booted monstrosities that we knew would come. Our throats were parched, our faces grimy and haggard. But our fingers were firm on our weapons, and if our attackers had water, it would shortly be ours . . .

I woke gasping and sweating. The sun was now high above; Joan was stirring and moaning restlessly beside me, her lips cracked and parched. Her skin was blistered where it was not covered by her clothing, and my own was in little better shape. I called out despairingly to a passing Arab woman . . .

10

Siege of the Pyramid

The gross Arab woman, dressed in filthy rags and with the flat nose and features customary to the Bedouin females, stopped and came towards me.

'The woman — ' I gasped. 'Can't you get her some water? We aren't supposed to die here — and she's in a bad way.'

She stared at me from beneath heavy brows, then directed her attention to Joan, who was now twitching convulsively, running her parched tongue over her cracked, swollen lips. Then she moved away again, and I groaned as I thought my plea had fallen on deaf ears. But within a few minutes she was back, bearing a rough clay drinking pot. She bent over the woman and touched her shoulder . . .

Joan's eyes opened, and she stared in anguish up at the woman; the Arab pointed to the pot she held then to Joan's lips, and I saw the look of eagerness spread across the latter's face. She opened her mouth as the woman tilted the pot — and a stream of burning sand particles trickled into her throat!

I cursed myself — I might have known it! That woman could beat the devil himself for cold-blooded cruelty.

Joan writhed and gagged, spluttering the sand out of her mouth, and the woman roared with harsh laughter, and tilted the pot again.

'You devil!' I cried angrily, my voice a mere croak. 'You filthy devil . . . '

I had directed her attention to myself, but at least I had spared Joan any further torture. She now came across towards me, pot in hand, face twisted into a cruel grin. With stubby fingers she forced my mouth open, and tilted the pot . . .

The sand was unbearably hot; it coursed into my mouth, setting me coughing and choking as it welled in the back of my throat. I coughed it out as she stood roaring with mirth, and where my throat had been bone dry before, it was now inflamed and irritated by hot sand.

But she hadn't finished yet; her fingers sought my lips again, to force them apart . . . and in desperation I sunk my teeth in her hand!

I regretted it at once; the look of sheer savagery which crossed her face unnerved me entirely. I watched, petrified, as she drew back her foot, and drove it into my groin . . .

Never have I known such agony in my life. I felt as if I was being wrenched apart, as if my whole body was splitting in two. I tried to clench my teeth, but her second kick drew from me what I can only confess (ashamedly) was a throbbing shriek of agony. I hesitated to think what would have happened had she worn shoes or sandals on her feet! From the corner of my eyes I saw Joan. She was horrified, staring at the scene, and two tears were trickling down her cheeks. As the woman drew back her foot for a third, kick, she cried: 'Oh, don't — please, don't!'

The third kick never landed; not because the woman heeded Joan's plea, but because the scene had now been observed, and a tall Arab strode rapidly over and sent a swinging blow to the side of the woman's head. She scuttled away, screeching foul words at him, and he looked down at me.

'My wife,' he said. 'She forgets she is here only to tend the cooking pot and do the work. You are thirsty?'

I croaked a hoarse assent.

'I will bring you water.'

He moved across to a tent, emerged with a large pot, then walked towards the oasis. This time it was no joke, and within a few more minutes water was coursing down my throat; it was warm and brackish — but I confess it was the sweetest liquid I have ever tasted. He allowed me to drink only so much, then served Joan in the same way. When he had finished there was still half a pot left, and this he threw over Joan and me impartially, cooling our sun-blistered bodies.

'I will bring you water again at sundown,' he told us. 'That will not be long now.'

I was taken aback by his apparent kindness; but, I reflected, quite a number of those fierce sons of the desert have, at times, suffered the horrible tortures of thirst. Possibly this man, remembering his own anguish, could feel pity for anyone in a similar state.

The drink and shower had revived us wonderfully, and we began to talk in low tones. Joan was still hopeful — she still clung to a belief that we might escape and prevent the massacre at Tarfa even now.

'We must, somehow, Colin,' she whispered. 'We know their plan can't be a success, but think of the poor people who'll die before they're put down.'

Not wanting to quench her hopes, I said: 'There may be a chance tonight, Joan. Try to save your strength in case.' But actually my own spirits were very low. I could see no prospect of our being able to break away from our cruel captors.

The sun set suddenly, and a half-twilight lay over the sands; before it was completely dark we were taken from our pegs, our hands bound before us, and thrown into a small, fusty tent. A gnarled Arab sat cross-legged inside the doorway on guard.

Hours crawled by, and gradually the

man's head sunk lower to his chest, the rifle dropped from his folded knees, and he slept. His snoring blended with the faint snoring from the tents about us; the camp was asleep.

Joan whispered: 'Now, Colin.'

'But we haven't anything to cut our bonds with,' I told her, after a glance round the tent.

'We have,' she whispered excitedly. 'When they searched me they missed a nail file — it's in the front pocket of my skirt. Can you manage to get through your ropes with that, do you think?'

A spark of hope flickered in my breast. 'We can try.'

I rolled nearer to her, so that with an effort I got my bound wrists close to her skirt pocket. My finger edged into the interior and touched a small pearl-handled nail file which, because of its size, had not been noticed by the Arabs who had searched us. I gripped it gingerly between thumb and forefinger, and drew my hand out.

The rest was not easy, but we managed it. Joan held the file as tightly as she could with her bound hands, and I sawed my bonds up and down across it. It took almost two hours, and once or twice we were forced to desist when our guard gave snuffling grunts or moved position slightly.

Finally I was three-quarters of the way through the rope — and a final jerk snapped it cleanly. I was free!

I untied Joan's hands first, then we both worked rapidly on the ropes about our ankles. I cautioned her not to move until the blood had been coaxed into circulation again, and we sat rubbing our legs energetically.

The flow of returning circulation made us wince with pain; but the knowledge that we were at least free helped us to bear this with a great deal of fortitude. At last Joan expressed herself ready to make the attempt for complete escape, and I eased myself upright. I crept across to the slumbering Arab; and before he knew what was happening, my arms were about his bent neck, and I *wrenched* . . . Then a sharp blow with my fist to the base of his skull, forcing his head upwards, snapped his neck cleanly and neatly. I had reason now to thank my unarmed combat training with the army.

I laid him gently down in a sitting position and seized his rifle and an ugly knife from his waist. Then I nodded to Joan, and she crept painfully across and joined me at the tent flap.

I moved aside the strip of goatskin and looked out. The camp was in darkness, slumbering soundly. From the right, by the oasis, came the whinnying of horses; and closely followed by Joan, I started to crawl in that direction.

There was a guard on the horses; we could dimly see him lying flat at the edge of the pool of still water, apparently filling a cup to drink. Joan remained motionless and I moved stealthily forward. It was essential that the man should be dispatched quietly and speedily before we could finish our plan of escape.

Once again I was thankful for my training in desert warfare. I had the man by the throat, his head forced down into the water and jammed in the mud on the bottom, without him making a sound. I sat astride his flailing legs, waiting, while bubbles rushed up and broke above the oasis, and the wild thrashing of his arms and legs stopped.

That done, I eased him bodily into the pool, stood upright, and choosing two mounts a little away from their fellows, unhitched them from the palms and led them silently round the oasis, away from the camp.

We did not risk mounting until we had put a huge sand drift between ourselves and the tents. We were not sure whether other guards had been posted about, and we could not afford to run any risks.

But at last we were astride the horses — saddleless, but on our way. It was rough riding across the desert wastes without saddles; but as we were both excellent horse riders, we were able to stay put and travel at quite a rapid pace. As dawn began to break again Joan reined in and said:

'This is where we branch off for Saqqara, I think, Colin. If I'm right, that clump of palms to the left is a small oasis called Kanor. I can find the way from here.'

'I can't go with you,' I told her. 'I must go back to Khufu and warn my friends about the attack. If they aren't warned they'll be butchered mercilessly. But you go ahead — and for God's sake get help there as soon as you can. If you aren't in time we'll try to hold out for a while.'

'Couldn't you all leave at once?' she asked.

'Not without the truck — and that's gone now. No, we'll have to hold the fort, I'm afraid. But hurry.'

I leaned over and kissed her on the lips; and then she was spurring in the direction of Saqqara, and I was speeding towards the east and Khufu, which she had told me lay almost in a straight line with my present course.

I must have lost myself in the wastes of the Libyan desert. For although Joan had said Khufu was only four or five miles from the oasis of Kanor, I was still travelling hard when the sun had risen halfway towards the midday point. I judged the time to be about nine o'clock, and now I began to regret my haste in not pausing at Kanor for a drink before riding on.

It could not have been long afterwards that I saw in the distance a large jutting mass of sandstone rock. It looked like the valley of the pyramid to me, and as I drew nearer I could see the two fellah still on guard before the tunnel entrance. I drew towards them and they welcomed me with glad cries. No one, they told me, had attempted to leave the tunnel.

In view of the fact that the Arabs might arrive at any moment, I decided they could not remain there. I dismounted, and between us we fought to push a great chunk of loose stone across the mouth of the passageway.

We had hardly completed this task when one of the fellah gave a cry, and pointed to the desert. A great rolling cloud of dust was approaching rapidly, and he said: 'Look, Effendi!'

'Not a sandstorm,' I said, and he shook his head.

'Horses, Effendi. A lot of them.'

I knew what must have happened: our escape had been discovered, and the Arabs had been riding hard after me. I breathed a prayer that they had not caught Joan; then, hustling the fellah before me, I raced across the hillock and into the valley.

It took only minutes to make the situation clear to Maurice and the others. They acted admirably, and on my suggestion of turning the pyramid into a fort, even the fellah forgot their fear and hurried about making hasty preparations.

When the first Arabs rode over the crest of the sandstone, they were met by a fierce hail of bullets from the top of the pyramid. We were in an unfortunate position, really. One side of the valley rose directly above the pyramid top, thereby exposing us to anyone gaining that summit. To combat this I positioned half our strength along the east side, their job being to kill instantly any riders appearing over the rise above them.

The first wave, not expecting any opposition, broke at once and spurred their mounts to safety again, leaving three dead. All told there must have been a hundred of them, and we numbered only about nineteen, counting the fellah and Rodney Strong, who was trembling so violently he could hardly hold his gun. Fortunately we had a good supply of ammunition, and were in no danger of running out.

Emergency has strange effects upon a man; every one of our little garrison — except for Strong whom I have already mentioned — played up like seasoned veterans. Even the old professor was gripped by the excitement of the fray and fired as fast as he could reload, scoring more than one bull.

The second wave came in about fifteen minutes; ordinarily the Arabs would have waited for dawn the following day, but since their scheme had to be put into operation that very night, they could not follow traditions. Around three-quarters of their force burst yelling across the valley, springing from all directions. The defenders at the east side did well, picking off every man to appear; and the second wave expended itself quickly. The dead and dying before the pyramid now numbered fifteen or sixteen, and five more had fallen from the east hill, one of them actually crashing onto the pyramid top itself.

Half an hour passed, and the next assault was more cautious; around thirty of the Arabs raced across the hill and began to circle wildly about our little fort, firing incessantly. One of the fellah went down, a bullet through his temple. Maurice grunted as a second bullet tore into his right hand. It was plain to me that eventually they would wear us down; and then I remembered something I had hitherto forgotten.

'Trix,' I called, 'you and I are going into the pyramid. We've got to find that storeroom and get a couple of machine guns up here. Are you game?'

He nodded, and I called for Professor Grimm. 'You take over, Professor. We're going to . . . '

I stopped speaking as there was a sudden chorus of yelling from outside the valley. The Arabs came riding over the hill in full force — but now they were firing *backwards*.

Then a glorious sight burst upon us. A solid line of native soldiery breasted the rise, advancing grimly, firing as they came. The white officer in charge rallied them on, his horse wheeling and turning just behind their lines. The dying Arabs fell right and left, their horses bolting madly across the sand.

We raised a feeble cheer ... and it ended in a cry of horror from Maurice. I whirled, and cursed myself for being so utterly stupid as to have neglected the passage into the pyramid from outside, for twenty Arabs were pouring out into the flat top, firing as they emerged from the various tunnels. Amongst them was Doctor Harmer, himself handling a rifle.

I raised my revolver, sighted, and fired. Harmer stopped, sank to his knees, and then fell full-length across the hot stones.

Most of our fellah had dropped their rifles on one or two of their number being shot down. And now, realizing it was hopeless, I followed suit and raised my hands together with the rest of them.

Harmer raised his head weakly from the ground, glared malevolence at me, and croaked: '*Kill!*' And the Arabs, ignoring our total lack of defence, raised their rifles to their shoulders, and sighted —

But the firing came from *behind us;*

not one of the attackers had time to pull a trigger.

We were saved — saved by the stern-faced native troops who swarmed over the parapet of the pyramid, and by Joan, who climbed anxiously up right behind them!

★   ★   ★

It was some time before we could complete the film *Flame of the Pyramids*. But at last it was done; and, as you know, it has won universal acclaim.

Maurice is firmly on his feet, and is well on the way to being one of Hollywood's biggest and best movie moguls. But strangely enough, he has never tried to make a sequel to *Flame of the Pyramids*. He claims he never will. It seems he's had quite enough of Egypt.

Joan, at my persuasion, no longer works for the Secret Service. Now she works for Maurice, and is his big star. And more than that, she works for me — as my wife.

The woman who wanted to rule Egypt languishes in some jail; Doctor Harmer

163

died where he fell on the Pyramid of Khufu; and Egypt has been freed of the Sons of the Sphinx, for its sons are no more.

I remember shortly after we had returned to Hollywood, Maurice dropped in to see us one night. 'You know,' he told us, 'I think they ought to give you people recognition for what you've done. You ought at least to get a medal out of it.'

Joan looked at me and smiled. I looked at her, then at Maurice. 'Maurice,' I said, 'we've got all we wanted out of that adventure. We've got something which is far better than any amount of medals — understand?'

He looked blank for a moment, then smiled. 'Oh, I see. Yes, I'm inclined to agree with you at that. We all got something out of it: I got a superb picture; Professor Grimm got the satisfaction of discovering the treasures in the queen's chamber; the fellah and Yusef got a nice reward for their services; Bob Lieberman got a job in Egypt — seems he likes it there; and Rodney Strong got a great deal of prestige which he *didn't* deserve!'

164

'And I got Colin,' smiled Joan.

'And Colin got Joan,' I finished. 'So no one can grumble.'

'Except Trix,' said Maurice. 'Trix didn't get a thing.'

'No, he didn't, did he?' I said. 'Poor old Trix. But think of the boasting he can do to his girlfriends . . .'

'Yes,' agreed Maurice. 'There's always that. Ah, well, I'd better leave you now — I see you want to be alone. But don't forget — when you're ready, there're movies to be made!' He dug in his pocket. 'Oh, yes, I almost forgot. Here's your engagement present. Thought you'd like it.' He grinned, laid it on the table, and hurried out.

We looked at it in silence for some moments. Then Joan said: 'Yes; I *do* like it. After all, it's what really brought us together, isn't it, Colin?'

And she was right: that little golden Sphinx with the chipped nose now occupies a place of honour in our drawing room!

Corpses Don't Care

1

Signor Valentini stepped from his car, regally adjusted his fur-collared coat, bowed to the cheering crowd, and strode to the portals of his luxury hotel which he was about to open officially. He glanced at its architectural majesty with great pride. It was here he hoped to spend his declining years. He intended to make people speak of the hotel not as the Superba, but as Valentini's.

With solemn dignity, Valentini inserted the golden key in the lock of the outer shutter, turned it, and grasping firmly at the ring on the lower end of the shutter — he was a vigorous man — swung it heartily upwards, revealing the hand-some, revolving entrance doors — and the frosty-eyed corpse which stared negligently out at him through the glass panels!

'*Sapristi!*' gasped Valentini. 'Who is this corpse? I not know him!' Then he fainted

169

into the arms of the two police constables who had been keeping the crowd in order.

When Signor Valentini had recovered from his brief swoon, the investigation began. The doors were revolved. The corpse fell aimlessly into the hotel from its section of the door. Signor Valentini, and the two constables who were supporting him, pushed inside.

'A tragedy,' moaned Valentini, clutching frantically at the sparse locks of hair curling about his ears. 'A calamity! Why should this happen to Valentini? Never, *never*, have I before been so humiliated, so . . . so upset. *Sapristi!* In *my* hotel — my *luxury* hotel! I am ruined!'

Meanwhile the constables, more concerned about the corpse than the Superba's reputation, had sent for Inspector Fermen of New Scotland Yard.

'Hmm,' said the inspector. 'You've seen the body, Valentini?'

'But yes, I have seen it. It is terrible. It is one of the directors — Mr. Haines.'

'But the constable said you declared you did not know the man.'

'I made a mistake. I saw him only the night before last. He was so happy then. The directors were all here. They dined in the Rosewood Room. It was a celebration to mark the end of their achievement. I, Signor Valentini, served them with food, leaving them the wine before I left the building.'

'Why?'

'It is my custom to retire always at midnight. You see, there was little more I could do here. The directors wanted to hold a private conference. I was asked to withdraw. Jules, my head waiter; Gaston, the head chef; and one of the kitchen maids stayed behind to attend to their wants.'

'I see. This was Saturday night. Were you here yesterday?'

'But no. It was Sunday, and everything had been prepared for the grand opening today, Monday. There was no one here yesterday!'

Fermen looked thoughtful. Finally he said: 'Then obviously this body was placed here after the directors left on Saturday, and before the opening today.'

He turned to the divisional surgeon, who had completed his examination. 'What's the verdict?'

'Poison. I can't yet say which, but it seems to have been an unusually quick-acting one.'

'Injected?'

'Not at all. As far as I can ascertain without a post-mortem, it was taken in some liquid or food. Notice the blue lips. I can't tell exactly when the man died, but I should estimate it as being more than twenty-four hours ago.'

'He could have been dead since Saturday night, then?'

'Quite possibly.'

Fermen returned to Valentini. 'How many directors are there?' he asked.

'There are six — now, alas, it is but five. Inspector, I beg of you to keep this matter quiet. My reputation, it will be *garbage* if this leaks out.'

'Where are the staff?' rapped Fermen. 'Surely you had no intention of opening the hotel without staff?'

'But no. They are all at the back door waiting to come in. I was to admit them immediately after the opening ceremony had taken place, and before the guests began to arrive.'

'Then be good enough to let them in now, and bring to me the staff who remained in attendance on the directors at the late supper last Saturday night. Hurry, man.'

Valentini, wringing his hands and moaning, scurried away. Within five minutes he was back again, together with three other persons. The four of them lined up as though they were waiting for tips.

'Now then, Valentini,' said Fermen, 'you claim that you left at twelve, and that these three people stayed behind?'

'It is the truth.'

Fermen let his glance wander over the three newcomers. Jules, the head waiter, was a surly-looking but quite handsome man, seemingly of French extraction. Gaston, the chef, was also French, equipped with a pair of comical side-whiskers and an immense moustache. The kitchen maid was a frightened-looking girl of about eighteen.

'You are the head waiter here?' demanded Fermen, addressing Jules.

'That is my profession, sir.'

'Will you be good enough to explain exactly what happened when Mr. Valentini left on Saturday night?'

'The directors were talking and joking, sir. I heard them mention with regret the absence of their chairman, Mr. Curtis Clayman. It would seem he was unable to join them because of a splitting headache. Then they noticed me standing there, called me over, asked me to bring some bottles of the finest wine, and told me I could go to my home. They said also that Gaston, the chef, could leave.'

'And who was to clean up the glasses and the table?'

'Alice, the kitchen maid.'

'That's right, sir,' chipped in Alice. 'I stayed here 'til after one o'clock, then I went in to clean the mess up what they left.'

'You saw the directors then?'

'Not an 'ide nor 'air of them. They'd gone, sir. I never 'eard them go out, but then, I was in the kitchen readin' *How*

174

True Was Her Heart. When I finished reading I went into the Rosewood Room. The lights was still burning, but there wasn't 'alf a tidy old mess. Glasses was overturned; three plates was smashed; chairs was knocked all over the floor, sir. I cleared it all up, washed everything, and put the chairs right. Then I switched off all the lights and went 'ome, locking the back door after me.'

'You washed the glasses?'

'Yes, sir. Spotless, every one o' them.'

'Sure you didn't leave one of them dirty?'

'Oh, sure, sir. I do me job right, I do.'

'I was afraid of that,' grunted Fermen. 'Very well, Alice. They had all gone — silently, leaving a disordered table behind. Anything else of importance to tell me? You are sure Jules and Gaston had left at that time?'

'Oh yes, sir. Jules went 'ome first after 'e'd brought the wine up, opened it, and taken it to them. Gaston went just after.'

Fermen turned to Jules. 'When you opened that wine, did you leave it lying about, Jules?'

'Yes, sir. It was left open while I prepared the bucket for it.'

'Then either of you three could have slipped poison into it?'

'But Inspector,' chimed the horrified Valentini, 'if the man was poisoned instantaneously, why did his friends leave him here? Why did not Alice discover his body? Surely the poison could not have been administered in the wine?'

'You think not?'

'I merely say: what about the other directors? Where were they when this poor man died?'

'Exactly. Where are they now, Valentini?'

The Italian shrugged expressively. 'Who can say? It is a fact that they should be here for the opening, but perhaps some mischance has delayed them. These things happen, Inspector, alas.'

'It would be some very strange mischance which could delay the remaining five, would it not, Valentini?'

'I do not know, Inspector.' Valentini tried to smile brightly. 'Perhaps they are at home now.'

'I doubt it. You see, Valentini, after their

176

dinner here on Saturday night, the directors did *not* return home. In fact, this morning four of them were reported by their wives as missing since last Saturday afternoon. The report came in just prior to my being called here to investigate this murder. I have no doubt the other two shared the same fate as the four, and possibly the same fate as this poor devil. This is mass murder! Your hotel is probably chock-a-block with corpses, Valentini.'

There was a soft thud, and Fermen said wearily: 'See what you can do for Valentini, Doctor. He's fainted again!'

★　★　★

Private Detective Bill Summers — stalwart, young, ex-commando — stood gazing at the magnificence of the Superba Hotel reflected in the eyes of his lovely young bride beside him. 'Ours is going to be the finest honeymoon ever,' he said.

'Is it, Bill?' Was her voice just the tiniest bit frightened?

'Anything wrong, Evelyn?'

'No, Bill. Of course not. What could be wrong?'

The honeymooning couple walked past the impressive commissionaires who stood statuesque at the door. They went through the revolving doors into a scene of hustle and bustle. Guests were arriving by the dozens. Page boys were sprinting up stairs with suitcases. Lifts were clanging, and the buzz of many voices filled the entrance hall.

Bill and Evelyn made their way over to the reception desk, and were confronted by a clerk with a harassed expression. 'We have arrived,' Bill said. 'But where, my good man — ' Here he wagged an admonitory forefinger at the clerk. ' — is the red carpet which should have been unrolled for us?'

The clerk sniffed and stared at them. Undeterred, Bill pressed on. 'Listen, we'd like a room for the week — '

'Sir, we've been booked up for months in advance. In fact, the only suite we have vacant is the honeymoon suite, and we can let that only to honeymoon couples.'

'Which,' said Bill with a smile, 'is

exactly what we are. Don't we look it?'

The clerk studied them again, and said: 'I must admit you do.' He smiled benevolently. 'Well, I should not recommend any young newlywed couple to stay *here*. It will not be very quiet for you, I'm afraid. You see, we've had a murder.'

'Murder?' Bill's eyes were like twin car headlamps.

'Yes, sir. Most regrettable. It happened this morning. A corpse was found stuck in the revolving doors when the place was officially opened. Grisly business! I expect you're glad I told you in time, eh, sir?'

'I am — *darned glad*,' agreed Bill. 'We'll *take* the suite!'

* * *

Signor Valentini, recovered from his hysteria of the morning, presided over the first gala opening of the Rosewood Room that night. The show must go on! Shortly he was to make a modest little speech, and then he would press a certain electric button. Trap doors in the ceiling would open, and fragrant rose petals would

179

flutter down onto the dancers and baptize the Rosewood Room.

The moment had arrived. Signor Valentini, after his preparatory speech concluded, depressed the button within the podium.

The trap opened. Rose petals began to flutter floorward. They were passed by a heavier object, which plummeted downwards into the middle of the dancers. There were a number of shrieks. The dancers flinched back as a corpse fell among them with a sickening crunch of bones. Rose petals went on falling round the dead man as a belated floral tribute. Valentini raised his hand to heaven and summoned his staff to deal with this new calamity. The diners were shuffled courteously from the room by the obliging waiters, and the dead man came in for some attention. Fermen, still on the spot, was rapidly examining the corpse.

'Whose bright idea was it to have those roses falling?' he rasped.

Valentini, between clutching at handfuls of his hair, admitted he was the genius responsible.

'Who put the rose petals in the trap?' bawled Fermen.

'I did, sir,' said one of the waiters, stepping forward. 'I put them up there late Saturday night, following instructions received from Signor Valentini. I *swear* when I put the rose petals in the trap, it was empty.'

The C.I.D. man was interrupted by a new arrival. Bill Summers touched the inspector's right arm. 'May I ask a few questions?'

'How in blazes did you get here?' the inspector roared. 'I told the waiters to move everybody out.'

'I'm a private detective on honeymoon,' Bill said breezily. 'I've been enquiring about this affair, and I'm definitely interested. It seems to me, from the facts I've heard, that this waiter wasn't mentioned as being present on Saturday night at all. There was supposed to be only the maid?'

'That's true enough, sir,' admitted the waiter. 'Possibly it slipped Signor Valentini's mind that he had instructed me to place roses above the dance floor of the Rosewood Room. And since I didn't

181

enter the kitchen at any time, the others would not have seen me. The moment I had completed the job I left the hotel.'

'Then how,' said Bill, 'did you get the janitor's key without entering the kitchen where it usually hangs?'

'I took it earlier in the day, sir, before I had obtained the rose petals. I should have placed them in position earlier, but the railway van was late, and the package had not arrived. The flowers came from the country, so that they would be specially fresh and fragrant.'

'And you replaced the key?'

'This morning, sir, after we had been admitted.'

The inspector blinked, speechless, and Bill eyed the waiter severely. 'You are *sure* of that? Remember that if what you say is true, the body could not have been placed with the rose petals until you had *replaced* that key. Therefore, if your statement is correct, the body was placed there sometime today *after* the opening of the hotel.'

'Not necessarily, sir. There is a duplicate key in the janitor's room.'

'Is that room kept locked?'

'No, sir.'

'One more thing,' said Bill, laying a comforting arm on the frowning inspector, who looked as though he was going to suffer an apoplectic stroke. 'Why didn't you mention your presence in the hotel last Saturday night when the murder came to light?'

The waiter looked confused. 'I — I — I wasn't asked. I thought that perhaps it would be as well not to mix things up.'

Or be implicated, thought Bill to himself.

Inspector Fermen, with a glare at Bill, snapped: 'Have you any objections to me getting on with my job now, young fellow?'

'None at all! Carry on, Inspector. Nice of you to humour me. Oh, just one thing. Has the corpse been identified?'

'Yes,' barked Fermen. 'It's another of the missing directors. A man named Lane. Is that all you want to know?'

'For the moment, yes.'

'Then get out and *stay out*! If you interfere in this case again, I'll send *you* some rose petals, but you won't be able to smell 'em!'

Bill exited, wondering just what exactly the inspector meant by that oddly cryptic remark.

* * *

'The whole thing's darned queer,' said Bill to Evelyn as they sat in the outer room of their three-room suite. 'First of all, six men hold a celebration supper in the Rosewood Room of their brand-new hotel. Then, within the space of about forty minutes, all six vanish into thin air! How? Where? And likewise, why? Today they start turning up in some darned queer places. Why must they turn up in *those* spots? Why weren't they, for instance, simply slung into the river, or generally kept out of sight?'

Evelyn yawned. 'Oh, Bill, let's not sit up talking. It's ten o'clock. Do let's go to bed, darling.'

'I don't like it,' said Bill. 'The mystery, I mean; not bed, dear. The bed's comfortable enough. Two corpses out of a possible six have turned up so far. Now the point is: where are the others?'

He stopped speaking as a rap came on the door. In answer to his invitation, Valentini, the manager, entered.

'Ah! You will forgive this intrusion, but I wish to speak to you, if I may?'

'By all means. Go ahead.'

'I understand you are a detective?'

'Thanks,' said Bill, grinning. 'I'd no idea my fame had spread to London.'

'No, no. It was you yourself who said so to the inspector. I admired the way you handled that waiter. You're a good detective, yes?'

'They don't come better,' admitted Bill ungrudgingly.

'*Sapristi!* It is well. It is this way, Mister — ?'

'Summers. This is my wife, Evelyn.'

'I hope so, Mr. Summers.' Without giving Bill time to assimilate this, Valentini hurried on: 'Mr. Summers, would you care to consider employment?'

'*On my honeymoon?*' echoed Bill in scandalized tones. '*Work?*'

'Of a sort, yes. The position is this: I

have neglected to provide a hotel detective on my staff. I had meant to do so later, but now that this has happened, the inspector is demanding to see my house detective. I took the liberty of informing him that you were the detective here. Now, Mr. Summers, if you'd please oblige — '

'But why? There's no law which says you have to have a detective in a hotel, is there?'

'Not that I know of. But it would be unthinkable that it should get out among my guests that Valentini had omitted to provide a house detective. They would feel unsafe. They would fear for their money, their jewels, their wives, their lives. Already I hang my head in shame to think that these unpleasant bodies should turn up here. Why must these directors die in *my* hotel, of all places, and in such ridiculous positions?'

'The indignity of their positions wouldn't worry them,' Bill said, smiling. 'Corpses don't care!'

'But I will be *ruined*. No, it must not be. You will accept the position, yes?'

Bill looked thoughtful, and then said:

'What about the wages?'

'I will pay to you a thousand English pounds every two weeks, and a bonus when you eliminate this dilemma. The hotel will provide you with apartments, and you will obtain your food free, in the staff quarters. Your work will be merely to mingle unobtrusively with the guests. As hotel detective, you will have a free hand. Inspector Fermen will not be able to stop you investigating the murders.'

'Very well, Signor. If I can help you out of a hole, I'll be tickled to death.'

Valentini beamed, seized the ex-commando by the temples and plastered a kiss on either cheek. 'Valentini is saved from ruin!' he exclaimed. 'I salute you, Mr. Summers.'

'Thanks; I'll be on the job first thing tomorrow morning. Good night. I think,' said Bill when Valentini had gone, 'we ought to be getting off to bed now. We've both had a long day.'

Evelyn kissed him lightly on the lips and made for the door of the bedroom. Bill said: 'I'll — er — hem — just finish reading an article in this *Police Gazette*, then I'll — hum — join you.' While he waited, he sang softly to himself: 'I ain't got no body . . . '

There was a sudden shrill scream from the bedroom.

'What's wrong, darling?' Bill, in two bounds, tore open the door and rushed inside.

'A body — *another* one!' shrieked Evelyn. 'I'd just opened the wardrobe, and *that* fell out!' Her pointing finger indicated a huddled heap at her feet. It was a fat, round little man. His face was pallid, like a gruesome death mask. His eyes stared sightlessly upwards. He was undeniably very dead, and incidentally, didn't make a very attractive corpse.

2

'You say you opened this wardrobe, looked inside it on your arrival, and found it empty?' queried Inspector Fermen wearily.

'We did more. We unpacked and hung our togs up in it,' Bill exclaimed. 'There was definitely no corpse there then. I take it this is yet another of the directors?'

'It is; Mr. Brown this time. It seems fairly clear, in the face of what you say, that these bodies have been put in position since the hotel opened. In other words, the man who's doing this has a stock of bodies somewhere on which he keeps drawing, so to speak. But why?'

'Why indeed?' echoed Bill, nodding. 'Personally I've a few ideas.'

'What are they?' queried Fermen, shooting a quick glance at him.

Bill smiled. 'I'd prefer to keep them to myself, for now.'

'Look here,' grunted Fermen. 'Valentini tells me you're the house detective. Is that so? It is? Well, then, why didn't you tell me that downstairs? And why are you occupying the bridal suite?'

'To your first question: Because you didn't ask me,' replied Bill. 'And to your second, because I'm a blushing bride — or rather, my wife is. We were married this morning.'

'But isn't it unusual for employees of a hotel to occupy bridal suites in that hotel?'

'It is. But then, this is an unusual hotel, and Signor Valentini is a warm-hearted old . . . er, gentleman. We are here at his invitation. He *likes* us. Young love and all that. You know, Inspector, I wouldn't be surprised if you were young once yourself.'

Fermen grunted and said: 'Well since you're the house detective, you'd better be in on the next move. I intend to search the hotel from top to bottom. I've sent for reinforcements, and they should be arriving at any minute. Or do you prefer to work alone?'

'Not at all,' said Bill light-heartedly. 'I'm no snob, Inspector. I'll be a bit embarrassed, but I don't mind being seen in doubtful company. Lead on, Inspector.'

'But Bill, darling,' gasped Evelyn. 'You *can't* leave me.'

'Absolutely not,' said Bill, planting a hearty kiss on her face. 'I'll be back long before the crack o' dawn, my love. Look after yourself.' Then he was gone in the wake of Fermen, and with an angry exclamation Evelyn threw a pillow from one side of the room to the other.

Meanwhile, a solemn party was forming down below for the purpose of searching the hotel from wine cellar to roof garden. Headed by the Inspector himself, closely followed by the keen-eyed and newly-appointed house detective, the party first visited the cellars. There was much of interest here, including several bottles of fine old burgundy. But there were no bodies.

'Anyway, I expect there's plenty of *body* in those bottles,' Bill observed dryly. Fermen groaned deeply and led the party up again to the ground floor, on which lay several rooms and a main dining hall. Here, too, nothing could be found, and

Fermen hesitated to disturb the guests at that time of night.

The first floor yielded nothing in the nature of corpses, but on the second floor a stout constable found the first body of the expedition — an unfortunate mouse, caught in a snap-trap in the janitor's cupboard.

Valentini, who was one of the party, said: 'Mouses! *Sapristi!* I am ruined if this leaks out — ruined! Never have there been mices in Valentini's hotels. Please — you will *not* mention this to anyone, gentlemen.'

'We aren't interested in *mice*,' retorted the inspector. 'And if I were in your shoes I'd worry more about the murders which have taken place here.'

'Inspector! The murders could be overlooked. But mice — ah! — unforgivable! Please not to mention it to anyone.'

The party pressed on, and Valentini took Bill by the arm and led him aside. He said: 'Mr. Summers, tomorrow you will move from the bridal suite into the onsite staffs' quarters. I am having rooms prepared for you.'

'Can't be done,' Bill told him regretfully. 'You see, we happen to be on our honeymoon, and in any case I've already told the Inspector you've lent us the bridal suite for the week. He admires you for it, Signor. 'Ah, yes,' he said, 'Signor Valentini is a great and noble man of generous heart. It is like him.' You wouldn't want to make him suspicious now, would you?'

Valentini groaned again and tore more hair. 'Very well, Mr. Summers; but next week, you must remove yourselves from that suite.'

It was several weary hours later that they reached the last floor. Discouraged, Fermen leaned against the wall and told his men: 'You can go now. Cleves and Vandon, Hawkins and Grissom, stay here and keep your eyes open. The rest of you report back to the Yard. Good night.'

The clatter of large service boots faded away down the stairs, and Fermen grunted: 'Well, that's that. We've scoured every possible place where a man might keep a few bodies, and we haven't found a thing.'

'Except a dead mouse,' put in Bill.

'Please,' begged Valentini. 'Please not to talk about the mouse, Mr. Summers. It was, after all, but a little mouse. Perhaps it had strayed in here accidentally.'

Fermen pressed the button of the automatic lift. 'Tomorrow I'm making a search of all the rooms, Valentini. I trust you will arrange that for me.'

'But Inspector Fermen, think of the scandal! Is it not bad enough already without having my guests disturbed?'

Fermen gave him a steely stare and said: 'I assure you your guests will be considerably *more* disturbed unless this case shows some clues shortly. If I have to root through every nook and cranny in the place, I'm determined to find those bodies.'

He pressed the button on the lift gates, and they slid aside. He stepped in and almost fell over the huddled corpse which lay on the floor of the lift.

'Ye gods!' raved Fermen. 'Another of 'em! This has gone too far. Four in less than twenty-four hours, and two more still to come. Where the devil are they hidden? Who's doing it? And how's he transporting them up and down a hotel of this size, full of people?'

Which was precisely what Bill was thinking. But his thoughts were much nearer the truth than the inspector's.

* * *

Jules, head waiter of the Superba, strode aloofly along the passage behind a serving trolley laden with an assortment of choice food.

It was the day after the opening of the hotel, and Bill Summers was trying hard to look like a house detective. He stared at Jules suspiciously, and with an elevated nose Jules passed on. Bill scratched his head elaborately and eyed Jules's retreating form with much displeasure. Then Bill turned and went to his own rooms, where Evelyn was seated, reading a magazine.

'I don't like that Jules chap,' observed Bill. 'Nor do I like the look of the cook, Gaston, or the kitchen maid, Alice. A cunning group, if you ask me. I wouldn't be a bit surprised if there wasn't some kind of a conspiracy going on.'

'Good gracious, Bill, you've been suspecting *everybody* you've seen ever since last night. You'll be thinking *I* had something to do with it next.'

'Did you?' said Bill with a smile.

'Of course I did! I simply adore hauling dead bodies all over the place, dear. Didn't you know it was one of my fascinating hobbies?'

'What I'd like to know,' said Bill thoughtfully, between kissing his wife, 'is why these dashed corpses are arranged to make dramatic appearances. I mean they've been found in revolving doors, flying from ceilings, in wardrobes, and in lifts. Why? What's the motive?'

'Can't you think of one, dear?'

'No. Can you?'

Evelyn lay back and yawned. She scratched the tip of one tiny ear and said: 'I'll tell you what I think. Having actually dated a reputedly *good* detective, my love, there's only one motive that I can think of. For instance, suppose someone wanted to ruin this hotel? Suppose they wanted to frighten the guests away? Wouldn't this corpse idea be the finest way of doing that?'

Bill sat up, and her legs bumped off his knee. He leaned forward and planted a resounding kiss on her lips. He said, with considerable excitement: 'Evelyn, I do believe you've hit something there. Of course, it would be one way of scaring away the guests. Twenty of them have already left so far, and when those other two corpses turn up, I wouldn't be at all surprised if the others didn't fold their tents and steal silently away without paying their bills.'

After kissing his wife again, Bill headed for the door. As he opened it, she wailed: 'Bill! You aren't leaving me *again*, are you?'

He struck a dramatic pose. 'Alas, duty calls. But I shall return, my love. Have no fear.'

'Well, you *needn't*,' she snapped. 'And don't try to be funny about it either, Bill Summers. Ever since we came to this wretched hotel you've done nothing but dash in and out of this room. You can stay *out* this time — all night.'

'But honey!' said Bill, hurt. 'You insisted on my taking the job, didn't you? You thought it was a stroke of luck.'

'I was being facetious! I didn't think it would mean we'd become practically strangers in a few short hours,' said Evelyn, almost crying. 'What kind of honeymoon do you think this is, Bill? Am I your wife, or are you married to those — those awful corpses?'

'A sticky thought,' said Bill, shuddering. 'Very sticky. But we'll make up for it, darling. I'll see to that. Now dry your pretty eyes, and trust me.'

'But I don't understand you, Bill. *When* will we make up for it?'

'As soon as I've nabbed the blessed murderer and found those two last corpses,' he told her, then jumped hastily outside and slammed the door as a large ornamental vase whizzed towards him. It shattered against the woodwork, and was followed by Evelyn's voice:

'Don't ever speak to me again, Bill Summers!'

* * *

'Never,' sighed Valentini, 'never has so great an indignity befallen me. To think that I, Valentini, should come to this. It is not credible. It is some 'orrible nightmare.'

'I wish to heaven it was,' said Fermen, as heartily fed up as the manager. 'Unless I get some action soon, the Yard'll want to know why they're paying me. What's that?' he asked suspiciously as the lights dimmed and a large upright box was wheeled onto the dance floor.

'Tonight's guest act, Inspector. I have engaged Maligna, the world's greatest illusionist, to give a performance. I had hoped his novel presence would bring back some of the patrons, but apparently they are too afraid.'

Fermen watched idly as Maligna the Great, tall and saturnine, appeared in a cloud of smoke. A wave of his hand, another flash and a cloud of grey fumes, and there appeared beside him his glamorous assistant. She smiled and bowed to the guests, who clapped half-heartedly.

'Ladies and gentlemen,' exclaimed Maligna, addressing the diners, 'tonight I

199

have brought for you the famous vanishing lady trick. Since I am working upon a dance floor, the possibility of trap doors can be ruled out. Also any member of the audience is welcome to inspect my cabinet here.'

As there were no volunteers, he went on: 'I will place the lady in the cabinet, then I will take the cabinet to pieces before your very eyes. The lady will be gone and you will not see her again until the end of my performance when I will reconstruct the cabinet and produce her from within.'

Fermen murmured: 'That's damned clever if he can do it.'

Bill, who had moved to the inspector's side, chipped in: 'He *can* do it. It's a trick, of course. He relies on the dim lights and the black drapes which are round the bandstand behind him. Inside the box is a jet-black cape to match the drapes. The woman steps in, dons the cape and goes right through the back. A couple of steps and she's hidden by the drapes until it is time for her to step into the box again. Naturally the audience are watching for a girl in white tights, and therefore they miss the faint black shape stepping back to the dais and the shelter of the drapes.'

'I get it — sort of optical illusion?' said Fermen.

Maligna was now speaking again: 'I will open my little cabinet, my friends, and you will see what is inside — or rather, what is *not* inside. You will please observe that the cabinet is completely empty!' With a dramatic flourish he flung the door open and stood back complacently, waiting for the audience to have seen the box was entirely empty.

He suddenly became aware that something had gone wrong. All he could see was an expanse of open-mouthed white faces in the gloom, staring towards his little cabinet. He thought, in momentary panic, that possibly the loose black cloak which the girl used for concealment was somehow visible to the diners. The magician turned, slowly, and stared into the cabinet.

There was something in there which under the spotlight seemed to shine with an evil white glow. It was a pallid, stricken face with cold eyes staring fixedly at the diners. Only the face glowed luminously. Just a dark shadow below the face indicated that the 'thing' had a body.

A sudden clatter of applause came from the audience. They thought it was an illusion. They liked it. But Maligna, who was nearer, could see the fixedness of that ghastly face, the unnatural glassiness of the eyes and the stiffness of the entire body. Drifting into awestruck mortification, and exclaiming in the dialect of his early 'Old Kent Road' environment, he said: 'Ruddy 'ell! Strahk me pink! It's a ruddy corpse!'

Fascinated, he put out his hand to touch the spectral ghoul. He tugged gently at the garment it wore, as though to see whether he had at last really performed a genuine magical feat.

The corpse came out with a rush and crashed onto the dance floor. The audience realized at last that it was no trick, but another dead body that had come to light. The weird circumstances of its appearance created panic among the guests. Women shrieked and rushed for the exit; men shouted aloud and crammed forward towards the floor. Maligna the Great stayed no longer. Magician's cape afloat behind him, magic wand clutched firmly in one hand, feet pounding the floor, he burst from the hotel and was last seen going strong in the direction of Battersea Power Station.

3

'One more corpse,' said Fermen bitterly. 'Just one more to come and they'll all have been found, or rather chucked at us. Then we'll have no chance of discovering anything at all. So far we've discovered exactly nothing. I can see myself demoted to a plain sergeant again before I'm through with this infernal case.'

Bill sighed, plugged a cigarette into his lips and said: 'You aren't the only one in danger of losing something. I'm heading exactly the right way to lose my wife. The last thing I heard from her was that she didn't ever want to speak to me again.'

'I can't say I blame her for that,' said Fermen gloomily. 'I've been speaking to you since I arrived here, and so far I haven't heard you utter one intelligible remark.'

You mean intelligent, *Inspector*, Bill corrected while biting his tongue. Considering the slights he'd unprofessionally directed at the inspector, he'd rightly deserved the barb in return. And frankly, it wasn't as though he'd made any progress, either! Still . . .

'But Inspector, I *do* have ideas now and then. In fact, I've spent all today putting them into practice. I took, as a starting point, the problem of how these corpses were being toted round. They aren't things you can carry under your arm like a set of golf clubs, y'know. There must be some conveyance which is used to carry them. I think I know what it is.'

'You do? What, man? What is it?'

'Let me take you for a ride, Inspector,' Bill quipped.

'Pardon?'

'The service trolleys,' Bill stated triumphantly.

'Service trolleys?' gasped the inspector.

'Exactly! You may have noticed the type they have here. Under the top tray there's a large sort of cupboard; quite large enough to hide a body.'

'Mmm, yes,' said the inspector doubtfully. 'But I've also noticed that inside that cupboard there are decanters and siphons so that any type of drink can be supplied by the waiter, if the customer asks for it.'

'I grant you that. But it wouldn't need much strength to empty the cupboard and stuff a body in, would it? You see, if the guilty person happened to be a waiter, there'd be no questions asked. Anyone who spotted him would naturally think he was merely carrying some ordered foods, especially if he had the top tray loaded with food and cutlery.'

The inspector whistled. 'I believe you're right, Summers. It's the only way it could be done, now I come to think of it. But it doesn't get us very much forrader. There are more than ten waiters on room service. Any of them might be the guilty man.'

'Granted. At the same time, all we have to do is to keep our eyes open, and when we see a trolley being pushed around, take a look inside the portable bar underneath it.'

'And when we've done that once or twice, the killer gets wind of what we're up to and stops using that method of transportation. That'll be a fine help.'

'In that case, don't search until you're

sure. Just watch from cover, and if a
waiter seems to be wandering round
aimlessly, pounce on him.'

'It sounds easy, but I'm afraid it won't
work out quite as well as you hope . . . All
right, have it your own way. I'm desperate
enough to try anything once.'

Bill nodded and left him. He now
intended to keep an eye open for any
suspiciously laden trolleys. He had great
faith in his idea.

He thought wistfully of Evelyn. What
would she be doing? Did she really mean
what she had said? Ruefully, he admitted
to himself that he had spoiled their
honeymoon. He'd make it up to her; but
the question was, would she let him?

He tried to justify himself. Evelyn had
known what he was when she first met
him, and he'd never given her any reason
to imagine that he'd change. When there
was a mystery hunt, Bill had to be in at
the kill.

He wandered towards the janitor's
office. There was another line of investigation he wanted to follow before he finally
started looking for that elusive corpse

carrier. He found two of the three janitors on duty, smoking and gambling round a small table. He inserted himself in their midst, drawing a chair up to the table and sitting down. They nodded cordially.

'New house detective, ain't you?' one asked.

Bill admitted it.

'Care for a game of cards?' offered another.

'I think not, thanks all the same. I thought you chaps might be able to lend a hand in this investigation.'

'If there's anything we can do, mate, just ask us.'

'Thanks. I want to know about that spare key to the janitor's cupboard on the second floor. There's supposed to be a spare here, isn't there?'

'There is. It's hanging on that hook over there.'

'I see. Was it there when you got here yesterday morning?'

'It was. An' it's been there ever since, mate. One of the three of us has been in 'ere all the time, so unless the killer 'appens to be one of us, it weren't that key as were used. Get it?'

'Are there any other keys which would open that door other than the one in the kitchen?'

'There's three master keys which opens any door in the hotel. Valentini's got one; Jules, the head waiter, 'as got another; and the fireman's got the third. Cripes, you don't think it was one of them, do yer?'

'I don't know. I'm just checking the possibilities, that's all; just wanted to know how many keys were in existence. But, of course, a master key solves the problem. It would open any door, you say?'

'Any door at all, mate. But it don't say that because them three blokes 'as got master keys, that they done it. Not by a long chalk. We was all 'ere for a week before the place opened, and a week would be time enough for anyone to 'ave 'ad a master key made from moulds.'

'That's right, of course . . . There's one other thing: how many of the staff knew about that late supper which the directors were to have?'

'I don't rightly know that, but not so

many, I reckon. In fact, I think only the kitchen staff and Jules and Valentini knew about it.'

'Thanks again. You've been a great help. You've helped to confirm a certain, albeit so far groundless, suspicion of mine.'

'Any time, mate. Glad ter be of assistance.'

The trio went back to their game, and Bill walked thoughtfully into the kitchens. The day staff had gone home, but he managed to find a chef's assistant who had been on duty the previous day. He showed Bill the key to the janitor's cupboard, which hung with a row of others on the nails near the exit to the hotel.

'I wondered if you could tell me anything about that key,' said Bill. 'Could you tell me if it was there when you came here yesterday morning?'

'I couldn't tell you, sir, but perhaps Gaston could. He's head chef. He keeps his eye on the keys more than I do.'

'Where could I find him?'

'He lives on the premises. I don't expect he'll be in bed yet. Go along the servants' passage, first right, up the stairs, and his room's number eight on the left. You can't miss it.'

Gaston, the French chef, was lying in shirt and waistcoat on his bed, reading a lurid novel. 'Come in, cocky,' he yelled as Bill knocked. Gaston, whose real name was Sykes, hailed not from the sunny continent, but from a fish-and-chip parlour just off the Lambeth Road. Off duty, he dropped his French airs and graces and became plain Joe Sykes.

'Oh it's you, cocky, is it? Wot d'yer want wiv me, nah? You think I've been mixed up in these 'ere murders?'

'No, I don't think that, Gaston,' said Bill. 'I just came along to ask you if you'd seen anyone tampering with the key to the janitor's cupboard on the second floor?'

Joe was thoughtful before he spoke. '*Non*, m'sieur — an' if you wants it in plain h'English, that means not on your ruddy life. Nobody tampered wiv that key. I happened ter be workin' alongside o' it all yesterday — Wait a minute,' he said, suddenly sitting up. 'Nah I come ter think of it, didn't the narks search the place this mornin'?' Bill nodded. 'Well,' went on Joe, 'Did they 'appen ter search be'ind the band dais?'

Bill sat up and took notice. 'What's back there, Joe?'

'There's like a passage, wot the band boys use when they comes and goes to and from the band room, wiv a flight of steps leading up to the back of the dais. Old Maligna's cabinet, wot 'ad the corpse fahnd in it, was there. I saw it m'self. In the middle of them steps there's a small door. Yer wouldn't never notice it if yer didn't know abaht it. S'matter o' fact, half the staff don't even know it's there. It was meant ter be used as a storage space when we got anything ter store.'

'What makes you think I might find something there?'

'I don't think yer might. I just think it'd be worth your trouble to try it. That's all. Seems like one o' the kitchen maids claims she was passin' there earlier tonight an' 'eard funny noises comin' from under the dais. She came back an' told me, but I thought p'r'aps she'd 'eard Maligna getting part o' 'is act ready. Now it strahks me p'r'aps it was 'is nibs 'awkin' a corpse out ter put inter Maligna's cabinet. He could 'ave painted that phosphorous stuff on it down there, too. It's a tip, fer what it's worth.'

'It's a damned interesting tip, too, Joe. I won't forget you for this. If I uncover the killer, I'm due for a bonus. I'll see you get your share.'

His pulse quickening with excitement, Bill hurried back along the corridor and down the stairs. When he neared the passage leading from the band room to the steps at the rear of the dais, he went more cautiously. From the Rosewood Room came the melody of the musicians who were still playing for the remaining patrons. After the removal of the corpse, the room had stayed open. Everything was functioning perfectly once more. But Valentini was still gazing heavenwards for strength. He had heard that half his remaining clients proposed to leave on the following day. At the moment he was prostrated with an attack of nervous hysteria in his room.

Curtis Clayman, the chairman of the board of (deceased) directors and the chief stockholder, had paid a visit, looking extremely worried. If the hotel flopped, he would be ruined. He had sunk everything into it. The shares he had issued would be worthless, because it certainly seemed that the hotel must fail.

Bill arrived at the steps which led to the dais. He paused a second near the wooden partition which separated the passage from the Rosewood Room. Then, stooping quickly, he slipped the catch of the door in the side of the steps, opened the door, and crawled into the dark recess. He could hear the strains of a hot rhythm, and the regular thump of the bandsmen's feet as they tapped their time out on the top of the dais above him.

He began to crawl about the floor, searching the space around him with an explorative hand. His fingers touched clammy coldness over the far side of the dais. Further investigation convinced him he had found the missing sixth director. The corpse was huddled stiffly in death.

Before he realized his luck, he heard the door in the wooden steps being cautiously opened. He stiffened, on the alert.

The door closed again, and the chink of

light was cut off. Then someone started to move silently across the space towards the last corpse.

The figure's stealthy movements drew nearer. Bill stood half upright, tensed . . .

A groping hand touched his face. There was a startled exclamation, and then the two men were fighting fiercely, rolling about beneath the dais, clawing, kicking, punching, biting. It was a savage, desperate encounter, with no holds barred. The murderer realized he had bumped into trouble and possible exposure. He had touched a living, breathing face instead of a corpse, and he was fighting tooth and nail in the darkness to preserve his identity.

Over and over they rolled. A hard, jabbing knee smacked into Bill's stomach. He doubled, groaning, but his fingers found a grip on the other's throat, and he pressed hard. His adversary shot his hands to Bill's features, and found his eyes. He began to gouge! Bill manoeuvred his right foot free, let go the man's throat and kicked blindly.

There was a shrill cry from the murderer. Enraged with pain, he sent two vicious blows to Bill's stomach, and followed them up with savage thumps to the face and head.

Bill felt himself weakening. Desperately he hung on. In a red haze of pain and punishment, he saw the sudden flash of a light, and thought it was in his own tortured mind and nerves.

Then the hammering figure was dragged away from him, and the tight grip of Bill's fingers were loosened gently from their hold.

Inspector Fermen had heard the struggle and had arrived just in time, armed with a flashlight and revolver.

★ ★ ★

'He confessed to *everything*,' said Fermen later, when Bill had been made comfortable in bed and was being fussed over by Evelyn. Her mood had changed to loving tenderness when she saw him carried up, streaked with blood. 'It was Jules! He's a Frenchman born and bred, but he came over to this country fifteen years ago, and has worked as head waiter in various hotels.'

'But what was his motive?' queried Bill.

'It might have seemed entirely inadequate to you or I, but with his notions of debts of honour, it would be quite sufficient to justify the extremes he went to.' The inspector explained weightily: 'You see, ten years ago Jules was to be married. He had saved up for the happy event, and at that time he chanced to wait upon Curtis Clayman — who, by the way, is now chairman of the board of directors of this hotel. Curtis persuaded him to invest all his savings in a company which he and six others were floating. He assured Jules that his money would be trebled in no time at all.'

'Tell me the old, old story,' said Bill.

'Well, it seems Curtis and his six now-dead cronies were in the habit of floating bogus companies, and yet keeping just within legal limits. Jules lost every penny, and when he told his girl she walked calmly out on him. He began to plan his revenge; and when he heard, ten years later, that the seven crooks were financing the new Superba with Curtis as main shareholder, he determined to murder them. To discover more of their personal habits, he got employment as head waiter here. Curtis had forgotten him after such a long time; and, to aid the deception, Jules had grown a beard and changed his name from Renard to Jules.

'The rest you know. As head waiter, Jules volunteered to stay behind and serve the seven at their celebration dinner. Only Clayman declined to appear due to personal reasons, and escaped his own death. Jules was the man who poisoned the wine. He was the man who, having ostensibly left for home, turned back and carried the six bodies into hiding under the dais. On Sunday he let himself into the hotel with his master key. He had been disappointed that Curtis, the chief malefactor, had stayed away from the late supper because of a bad headache, but he had thought of an even more fitting plan to take his revenge on him.'

'I think I can guess what that was,' Bill said. 'His idea was to ruin the hotel and Curtis with it. Unfortunately it would have destroyed Valentini, an innocent man in this matter. Jules — or Renard, rather — knew Curtis had sunk his entire fortune into the hotel — and had borrowed heavily, too!' The inspector's brows raised upon this slight revelation. Bill pressed on. 'These things get round among the staff of a place like the *Superba*, where there are *plenty* of keyholes.'

'That makes sense,' said the inspector, nodding in agreement. 'So Jules sneaks in on Sunday and props the first body in the revolving doors, ready for the big opening ceremony on Monday. He reckons that will be a real good send-off. Later, with the aid of his master key and a service trolley that had an empty cupboard under the top tray, he was able to arrange the other corpses around the hotel one at a time. He nearly succeeded, too. One more corpse would have ruined this place completely.

'But you prevented it, Bill. Valentini holds himself in your eternal debt for saving his reputation. As a matter of fact, he asked me to tell you that before you take up your duties as permanent house detective, he wants you and your missus to spend a whole month as free guests here. That's his honeymoon present to you. There'll also be a cheque placed with the cashier for you as a small token of their esteem, as the saying goes.'

Bill murmured, 'Well, it looks like I'll be sharing a piece of that token with a man who provided me with a certain tip.'

Smiling, and having said his piece, the inspector backed out discreetly.

Bill put his arms around Evelyn. 'Now are you on speaking terms with your husband, darling?'

'I'd rather we kissed than talked,' she sighed happily. 'Six murders are enough for any girl's honeymoon. For mercy's sake don't rush off again, Bill.'

'Not on your life. You and I have got a lot of love-making to catch up with during the next month — and then some!'

THE END

We do hope that you have enjoyed reading this large print book.

Did you know that all of our titles are available for purchase?

We publish a wide range of high quality large print books including:
Romances, Mysteries, Classics
General Fiction
Non Fiction and Westerns

Special interest titles available in large print are:
The Little Oxford Dictionary
Music Book, Song Book
Hymn Book, Service Book

Also available from us courtesy of Oxford University Press:
Young Readers' Dictionary
(large print edition)
Young Readers' Thesaurus
(large print edition)

For further information or a free brochure, please contact us at:
Ulverscroft Large Print Books Ltd.,
The Green, Bradgate Road, Anstey,
Leicester, LE7 7FU, England.
Tel: (00 44) **0116 236 4325**
Fax: (00 44) **0116 234 0205**

THE WHITE LILY MURDER

Victor Rousseau

When New York department store magnate Cyrus Embrich is found stabbed to death at his office desk, the police have little evidence to go on. Embrich's secretary reveals that her employer had been in fear of his life, and in the event of anything happening to him, he had asked her to call in the famed private investigator 'Probability' Jones to assist the police. Aided — and at times led — by his able assistant Rosanna Beach, Jones finds himself caught up in the most complex and dangerous case of his career . . .

FIRE ON THE MOON

V. J. Banis

On vacation at her Aunt's villa in Portugal, Jennifer is attracted to both Neil and Philip Alenquer, two brothers who live in an old castle overlooking the sea. But Jennifer soon senses that something is wrong, though it is not clear where the intangible clues are leading. Words left unsaid; the burntout shell of a cottage; terror in response to the recitation of a poem; gunshots on the beach. It is a mystery with potentially deadly consequences, as Jennifer and her aunt learn when an arsonist sets the villa alight . . .

SINISTER HOUSE & OTHER STORIES

Gerald Verner

Whispering Beeches stands vacant, well back from the roadway, almost hidden by the thickly growing trees that give it its name — though since its owner, Doctor Shard, was murdered by an unknown hand three years ago, it has locally been known as Sinister House. One night, noticing a light in one room, newspaper reporter Anthony Gale enters through the open front door — only to stumble over a man's body lying stark and rigid, with a gaping throat wound! Four tales of mystery and the macabre from veteran writer Gerald Verner.